# Pressure

*A Best Friend Brother's Workplace Romance*

Pierce Motors
Book 2

Chiquita Dennie

304 Publishing Company

Editor: Brandi Zelenka My Notes In Margin

Final Proof: Baldwin Editing Services

 Created with Vellum

# Latest Releases

**Series**

## Struck in Love

The Early Years-A Prequel Short Story
Ruthless:Antonio and Sabrina Book 1
Savage: Antonio and Sabrina Book 2
Beastl: Antonio and Sabrina Book 3
Captivated By His Love:Janice and Carlo
Brutal: Antonio and Sabrina Booke 4
Redemption: Antonio and Sabrina Book 5

## Heart of Stone

Broken, Book 1 (Emery & Jackson)
A Valentine's Day Short Book 1.5 Emery & Jackson
Rebirth, Book 2 (Jordan and Damon)
Reveal, Book 3 (Angela and Brent)
Bottoms Up Book 3.5 Jessica and Joseph Short
Renew, Book 4 (Jessica and Joseph)

## Cocky Billionaire Boys

Cocky Catcher (Cocky Billionaire Boys Book 1)
Bossy Billionaire (Cocky Billionaire Boys Book 2)

**The Fuertes Cartel**
Stolen (The Fuertes Cartel Book 1)
Saved (The Fuertes Cartel Book 2)
Betrayed (The Fuertes Cartel Book 3)
**Carrington Cartel**
Torn: The Carrington Cartel Book 1
Claim: The Carrington Cartel Book 2
**Something**
Something Gained: A Romantic Comedy Book 1
Something Earned: A Romantic Comedy Book 2
**Pierce Motors**
Refuel: (Pierce Motors Book l)
Pressure: Pierce Motors Book 2)
**Summer Break**
Summer Nights: (Summer Break Book 1)
**TN Seal Security**
Aydin: Book 1
Nasir: Book 2
Nicco: Book 3
**Standalones**
Until Serena(HEA World Novel)
Temptation
She's All I Need
I Deserve His Love
Mutual Agreement
Scoring with Sadie
Exposed (A Bodyguard Novel)
Love Shorts:A Collection of Short Stories
Red Light District(A Fantasy Romance Short)

# Note From Author

This was originally published in 2020 as part of a fanfiction from Driven KB worlds that includes your fan favorites, Reece and Cyrus. Now the project is revamped and republished with new characters, but the same story of racing world. I hope you enjoy and continue to follow me for more updates.

# Introduction

Grab some wine and get ready for more spicy, sinful, sexy romance.

Are you signed up for my newsletter?

Join today and find out all the latest in new releases, contests, giveaways, sneak peeks and more.

www.chiquitadennie.com

# Author Inspiration

"Focus on your passions and don't let the negativity distract you."

—Chiquita Dennie

# Disclaimer

# Character Interview: Malik Pierce

Today ladies and gentlemen, we have the Vice President of Pierce Motors, and potential CEO if the rumors are true about Jackson Pierce retiring in a few years. Malik Pierce is sitting with us today. We're discussing his journey in the latest release from author Chiquita Dennie. Welcome to our new installment of interviewing our characters. We look forward to many more and love hearing your questions.

**Interviewer:** So happy you've joined us today. I know you're a busy man so I'll get right into the questions so readers can start reading about your journey. How do you feel about your story being told?

**Malik:** The author saved the best for last.

**Interviewer:** How did Sarai become attached to your campaign? We've seen her in a few shots at your campaign stops.

**Malik:** Sarai does work as publicist and brought in exposure to Kash's career. I wanted the same thing for our brand.

**Interviewer**: What would you say is the good and bad of running a billion dollar business?

**Malik:** The good is being able to see your vision come to life. The bad is that everyone has a say about your vision.

**Interviewer:** In the past you've been known as a playboy. Has this changed?

**Malik:** I don't speak on my private life.

**Interviewer:** I hear you're working alongside Sarai and Kash, is this true?

**Malik:** You have to read the book and find out.

**Interviewer:** Seems that the media implied you are a playboy.

**Malik:** No comment.

**Interviewer:** For readers that want to know if you've found love in this story, can you give us a hint?

**Malik:** I met my match.

**Interviewer:** Can you give us more details on your plans for Pierce Motors, since we can't get any hints on your love life?

**Malik: Be ready for more to come in the future.**

**Interviewer:** Can you give us one spoiler?

**Malik: One spoiler will ruin the fun.**

**Interviewer**: Tell us your favorite driver besides your sister?

**Malik: Cyrus is pretty high on my list.**

**Interviewer:** I know I speak for all the readers when I say that we appreciate you for hanging with us today. Readers enjoy and let us know how Malik fairs in this new release.

# Synopsis

***Pressure* is a hot, enemies-to-lovers romance, contemporary romance.....**

Falling for her best friend's brother was the worst and best thing Sarai could've done....

Malik Pierce is next in line to become the next CEO for a billion-dollar racing company. His family has groomed him for this position and their high expectations come with the privilege. He should be over the moon but instead the weight of a cheating scandal weighs heavy on his mind and his reputation.

Sarai Lambert left her home town to pursue her career and her dream of finding the right man. Now she's been handed both. Malik is everything she's ever wanted, minus the scandal that is slandering his name and threatening her dreams.

***Can Malik and Sarai find a way to make it work, or will Malik's problems tear them further apart?***

# Chapter One

## Malik

I walked into my office and slammed the door. Pissed wasn't the word I would use for the amount of stress I was under. Jackson and I had a meeting where he basically named me to take over as CEO in a year or two because he wanted to spend more time with his family. I never wanted this life for myself as Vice President of Pierce Motors because of what I would have to live up to in order to fill his shoes. To my parents, family, and friends, Jackson was the perfect businessman, husband, father, and friend. I was always the troublemaker, never really being a one-woman type of man, wanting to be a sports agent like his friend, Damon. Since my college career ended with a leg injury, I couldn't play basketball anymore, so I eventually changed majors in college from sports medicine to business as an acquisition to give in to my family's wishes. I loved my family, don't get me wrong, and I knew they loved me, but being the middle child came with big responsibilities. My older brother, Eddison Jr., was a reporter with a wife and two kids and my little sister, Arianna, was the starting driver for our team, married with one kid to the other star driver, Kamden "Kash" Coleman of Cyrus Premier Enterprises. I took my jacket off and sat down, leaning back in my chair, and looking at the ceiling. I heard a knock on the door and debated if I wanted to let them in or not. A second knock came, and I figured my secretary was about to bust in if I didn't allow her inside.

"Come in!" I called out.

The door opened and Kendra walked inside with an annoyed look across her face.

"Whatever it is, leave it on my desk," I said as I sat up to turn on my computer.

"What's your problem?" Kendra spat with her hands on her hips, head tilted to the left, and a furrowed brow. Kendra was older and I looked at her like she was an aunt. The one who thought she could tell you what to do with your life and give you unsolicited advice even if she didn't do the right thing.

"I'm working. How can I help you?" I asked as I clasped my hands together.

"See, your energy is all off, I don't do bad energy. Let's try this again. Close your eyes," Kendra stated and closed her eyes.

"Kendra, what do you want?" She opened one eye and glared at me. "Are you serious?" I asked.

"Fine, but you'll be asking me later how to get rid of bad energy in your life," Kendra informed me and sat down in the chair in front of my desk.

"I just left a meeting with Jackson and he wants me to take over," I replied.

"That's good, right? You'll be CEO one day and I'll be the assistant to the CEO." Kendra clapped her hands in excitement.

"I wasn't expecting to be in this role that long, Kendra. Besides, you barely work as the VP's assistant. How would it look if the CEO's assistant was constantly late for meetings and taking extra-long breaks?" I joked.

Kendra waved me off.

"You know I take care of my niece and nephew. Don't play, Malik."

I nodded in answer. She wasn't all that bad besides her knowing everybody's business at the company and taking extra-long breaks. Kendra was a great assistant and kept me on my toes. Also, it helped that she was married to our older cousin, BJ. They're both in their late forties and had a daughter who was now in college.

"What did you need anyway?" I questioned.

"Ooh...I wanted to tell you that Cyrus called, and he wants to meet with you about doing another charity race," Kendra advised.

The last charity race ended with my little sister in the hospital because a scorned team member and ex-lover of Kash's sabotaged her car. I was so pissed. I never wanted them to date in the first place because I knew how women could be, not to mention men. I'm a perfect example of a guy who will tell you straight out I'm not looking for a long-term relationship.

"When does he want to meet? I'm not sure about another charity race," I replied.

"That was a year ago, Malik, you have to move on. Arianna and Kamden are good."

"I know, it's tough because she's the baby of the family and we could have lost her because of his bullshit."

"Well, the culprits are in jail and you need to focus on this charity race and the upcoming deal that Jackson wants you to look into for Pierce Motors," Kendra reminded me.

I spearheaded getting Pierce Motors apparel secured in a major US and International merchandising deal that could bring in another billion dollars the first year with Arianna as the spokesperson. She was a young woman under twenty-five, had a huge social media presence, her own style, plus she was a celebrity athlete married to another celebrity athlete and they both had global appeal. Everybody said she could be up there with the great female athletes in a few years.

"Let Cyrus know I'll meet with him this week."

"Good, the next agenda is you hiring an intern," Kendra stated.

"I don't need an intern. I got you," I said and smirked. Kendra flipped me off and I burst into laughter.

"I'm too busy as it is, Malik. You need an intern and I have the perfect person for you."

I groaned not wanting to deal with interviewing another person. Kendra didn't even interview, she just said she was my new assistant when we talked at a family dinner and I came into work the next day and she was sitting at the desk.

"Who?" I asked.

"You promise not to get upset?" Kendra asked and already I was feeling agitated.

"Who, Kendra?"

"Asia Lambert," Kendra whispered.

Not hearing her clearly, I leaned closer to have her repeat the name. "What was that name again?"

Kendra huffed, crossed her arms, and repeated herself. "Asia Lambert from Cyrus Premier Enterprises."

"No," I said, refusing to deal with anyone with the last name Lambert.

"Listen—"

I held my hand up to stop her from talking. "No," I repeated.

"Cut me off again and see what happens," Kendra said.

Suddenly, there was a knock at the door, and we both looked up to see a young woman standing there.

"Hi, am I too early?" She asked, cheesing hard.

Already feeling like this was a setup, I groaned, then reminded myself to have a stiff drink and a woman later today to help relieve this stress. The woman standing at my office door didn't look over twenty with a short bob, long tight pencil skirt, big wide eyes, and long eyelashes that didn't look good on her. I didn't discriminate against women who looked good with or without make-up, but some of them went overboard, like the girl standing in front of me with a shit ton of make-up caked on her face and a white blouse that didn't leave much to the imagination.

"You're right on time, Asia." Kendra jumped up, extending her hand for Asia to shake.

I leaned back in my chair, waiting for Kendra to introduce us.

"You must be Malik Pierce?" Asia asked.

"I am," I replied, standing up and smoothing my shirt.

"Where are you going?" Kendra questioned.

"I have a meeting; you can handle this," I answered.

"Malik, she's your intern," Kendra snapped.

"You hired her, and I need to go meet with the marketing department and my lawyer," I informed her. I grabbed my jacket and cell phone, checking messages, and glanced up to see Asia biting her bottom lip.

"Will you be back today? I've given her a tour, but I needed to get a list to Reece of the guests we wanted for dinner," Kendra stated.

"I'll let you know after I meet with Canon and Margo," I told her.

She nodded and followed behind me as I left and walked down to the marketing department to Canon and Margo's office. Being the VP left very little time in my day, and everyone wanted my time. Checking my watch, I saw it was ten till eleven. I told Canon I wanted to meet at noon, but plans changed now that word would spread about me taking over. Canon was one of my best friends that I hired to help oversee and bring fresh ideas to the brand of Pierce Motors. We met in college and pledged Kappa Alpha Psi members aka NUPE, known as the pretty boy crew, and ended up being roommates. He'd calmed down since then and settled in as a father and husband, while I still ran the single life and had no plans of becoming committed to any woman. I pushed the door open as Kendra and Asia walked past toward the mail-room. I needed to make a note to find out who referred her to my department, young girls like her only wanted to get a check and not put in the work. I complained about Kendra a lot, but at least she got her work done and took a lot off my plate. I knocked on Canon's door and he said, "Come in," and I nudged the door open, seeing Margo already there.

"Perfect timing," I said.

"Wassup, Malik, I thought we had a meeting at noon?" Canon asked.

"We do, or we did. But plans changed. I have to meet with my lawyer." He glanced up at the knock at the door.

Sarai Lambert, the Publicist for Cyrus Premier Enterprises and The All Hands Home, stepped inside and her smile dropped when she noticed me. I didn't know what that was about because I barely spoke to her. What was weird was the hairs on my arms itched beneath my cotton shirt. I'd never had the type of reaction before.

"Hi Sarai," Margo said.

Sarai played with her cell phone. "Hey, Margo, I came to talk with Canon about something," Sarai mentioned.

"We're in a meeting," I said as an icy glare shifted back at me.

"I'm not stopping you," Sarai retorted as she walked over to Canon.

"What did you do now?" Canon, who was standing at the table next to Margo with documents spread out, joked.

"Nothing this time. Jackson named me CEO once he retires, so I need to go talk with my lawyer and see the paperwork."

Canon slapped hands with me, and Margo hugged me.

"I heard and I'm so happy for you, Malik. You deserve the position," Margo stated.

"Doubt I deserve it but can't turn it down when your big cousin puts the weight of the world on your shoulders," I commented, and they both looked at me in understanding of carrying on traditions in a family.

"Canon, do you have the budget for Arianna and Kamden's photoshoot?" Sarai asked.

"I was here first," I said.

"My topic is time sensitive," Sarai responded, turning away from me.

"So, what do you have here?" I pointed as I saw sketches of Arianna and the layout for a merchandising campaign, ignoring Sarai. Both Canon and Margo peered at us in shock.

"Margo came up with a few designs and one-line hooks. I know you wanted to have this done before the charity race but we'll need more time," Canon said.

"How much time?" I asked, crossing my arms.

"Sarai, I can help you in a few minutes. This was a scheduled meeting," Canon replied.

He rubbed his beard in thought.

"Fine, but I want double the budget than last time." Sarai shoved her hands in her pockets and walked out.

I chuckled as she left annoyed.

"Malik!" Canon yelled, and I whipped my head around to face him.

"At least a month, we knew this was a year in the making. But with everything that happened with Arianna from the crash, we stopped production on the shoot," Canon reminded me.

"I hear you, let me talk with Jackson and see what he says. How much are we talking about with regard to the budget?" I questioned.

"At least fifty million, minimum," Margo told me.

"That's for just the US? What about the international market?"

"It could go as high as two hundred million," Margo said.

I sighed and started thinking of ways to get Jackson to agree with the ideas.

"All right, send me over everything in bullet points so I can get Jackson on board with your vision."

"Sounds good. What are you doing for lunch?" Canon questioned, helping Margo to roll up the paperwork.

I shrugged not even that hungry after having a big breakfast that Cicely made and left for me. She worked for the entire family and finding out she was hired by Kash last year pissed me off, and I wondered if she had anything to do with them dating or if it was just a coincidence.

"I need to meet with my lawyer. I can probably push it back if you want to grab something really quick," I said.

"We can go to Sonny's. They have daily specials and I can get a sub," Canon stated.

"That's cool," I replied.

"Margo, you want to come?" Canon questioned.

Margo waved us off and walked toward her office next door.

"Who's that?" Canon asked, pointing behind me. I turned and noticed Asia and Kendra talking with another assistant in the office. All of the offices had clear open doors and windows. Nothing was off-limits unless it was Jackson's or my office with wood doors and soundproofing.

"That's my new intern," I answered. Canon whistled, shaking his head.

"Nothing is going to happen there," I told him.

"She's trouble," Canon said.

I turned back to him. "I know."

"Let's go so you can give me the rundown on this new intern." Canon grabbed his jacket and opened the door to leave, telling his secretary he'd be on call if it was an emergency. I followed behind and glanced up to see Asia staring at me again. The elevator dinged and the doors opened. I stepped on and Canon followed. I slid my hands in my pants, already feeling overwhelmed with the workload.

# Chapter Two

## Malik

We ordered our food and I sat back in the booth watching as people came and went as Canon talked on the phone to his wife. Gabriella worked as a chiropractor, and they had three kids. I was their godfather, and I took that role seriously. She was always annoyed because I spoiled them every time I saw them. Canon hung up the phone and sighed in frustration.

"What's up with Gabriella?" I asked as the waitress dropped off our drinks and appetizers. The place was normally crowded since it was in the middle of the business district in downtown L.A. They did a lot of celebrity events here and held business meetings. The paparazzi loved stalking the place; like right now I could see three cameras taking pictures of two high-profile actors sitting in the corner. I was used to this life because of my family, but the constant hounding and demanding to open up our lives was aggravating.

"Here you go, Malik. Do you need ketchup?"

Lyndsey asked. I came here often during the week, so they knew me by name.

"Sure," I said, picking up the steak and cheese melt, taking a huge bite out of the sandwich. My phone vibrated and my lawyer said okay about moving the meeting to after my lunch.

"Here you go," Lyndsey said, and I took it out of her hands as she smiled. I winked back at her and she giggled before swishing over to another table. I knew my appeal to women as a thirty-year-old single male. I had my hair in a low-cut box fade, stood around six-three, and had an athletic build from my basketball days. All the women loved my lips and my smile could turn on anyone, especially if they were mad at me.

"You sleep with her?" Canon asked, motioning toward Lyndsey.

I shook my head and wiped my mouth with the napkin. "Nope, I'm just friendly."

Canon groaned, rolled his eyes, and I chuckled at his expression.

"The women love me, what can I say?"

"You need to settle down with one woman," Canon said, taking a bite of his meatball sub.

"Don't speak that on me. I'm good on my own," I answered.

"The right woman comes along and you'll change your mind."

"I doubt that," I said as I heard someone yelling. I glanced toward the entrance and noticed Asia standing next to the last person I expected to see here. She was looking sexy as fuck and I hated to admit it but if she gave me a chance, I'd probably have a one-night stand with her, but her attitude was so over the top that I'd need her to leave right afterwards.

Our eyes connected and a scowl came across her face. She ended her call and put her phone in her purse as the hostess walked them over to Lyndsey's section.

"Hey, Malik," Asia called out and waved.

Canon took a sip of his water and looked over at the voice calling my name.

"Asia, we don't have all day," Sarai said.

"It's my boss, Sarai," Asia replied, rolling her eyes.

"What's up, Sarai?" Canon questioned, waving in her direction.

Sarai waved back. "Hey, Canon."

"Is he the only person you see?" I demanded.

Asia narrowed her eyebrows before she glanced at Sarai then me.

"Don't start, Malik. I'm not in the mood. Asia, you wanted to have lunch, right?" Sarai gestured to the table.

"Yeah," Asia answered.

"Then come on because I have a meeting right after," Sarai spoke, picking the menu from the table, effectively dismissing me.

"You look beautiful today," I said to piss her off and she flipped me the middle finger.

Sarai and I had always had the type of relationship where we worked together if we had to, but we'd both prefer not to be in the other's presence. She was too stubborn, always had to be right, and never shut up. I'd told her many times she pushed my buttons on purpose to get a reaction. I could see in her eyes she wanted to curse me out for fucking with her in public.

"How do you two know each other?" I questioned Asia.

"She's my cousin," Asia stated as Lyndsey came over to take their order.

"What's going on with you and Sarai?" Canon inquired, taking another bite of his sub.

I grabbed the glass of water and took a sip as Lyndsey walked over to our table, placed the check down, and took my empty plate.

"Nothing. Sarai's not my type."

"You mean the type that won't put up with your bull-shit one-night stands or on-call dates," Canon teased.

I checked my watch and saw it was going on one fifteen. I still needed to meet with my lawyer, so I reached into my pocket and grabbed my wallet, taking out forty bucks and placing it on the table.

"You paid last time. I got this one." Canon picked up the money and tried pass it to me. I held my hand up, stopping him.

"Nope, keep the change for my godkids," I told him.

"Gabriella's going to kill you about constantly giving them money." Canon chuckled and left another twenty on the table and stood up.

"Tell her it's for their college fund," I joked then glanced over at the loud laughing coming from Asia's table. The owner and Lyndsey said goodbye to me, and I moved my eyes from the pair at Asia's table and motioned bye before I pushed through the front door. I shook hands with Canon and caught a cab to head to my lawyer's office.

* * *

Thirty minutes later the cab pulled up to the massive building. I saw it was going on two in the afternoon and I usually stayed at the office until four or five. Stepping out of the cab, I left him a fifty-dollar tip and shut the door. I nodded at the doorman as he held the building door open, and I walked inside. Our family was a longtime client of Jameson Stapleton, he handled everything from my parents to my sister's and brother's affairs. Not having to wait to sign in, I strolled to the elevator and pressed the button for the top level. The doors opened and I hit the twenty-third floor for the partners' floor. My phone vibrated as the doors closed. I pulled it from my pocket and saw a message from Kendra stating Asia was all set up with a desk and phone line. She had also sent my schedule. As I stepped out of the elevator, I messaged that I would be back in an hour or so for a meeting with them both.

I pointed toward his door as his assistant motioned me to go ahead and I tapped lightly making sure not to see anything surprising. Jameson was finishing a call and I marched toward the chair in front of his desk and unbuttoned my jacket.

Jameson said goodbye and reached out to shake hands.

"I talked with Jackson already," Jameson told me, pulling out my file.

"I figured he would have run through everything with you," I replied.

"The position is huge and can bring a lot of money your way," Jameson said and passed the documents toward me. I flipped through the offering of CEO in two years and the bonus expected upon taking over the reins.

"The money's not the issue."

"What's the problem?" Jameson questioned.

I ran a hand down my face.

"I question if this is what I want, the pressure to live up to my family's name and business."

"You're good at what you do, Malik. The amount of money from sponsors that want to invest in Pierce Motors and having Arianna as the lead driver for the company shows in the increase in ticket purchases."

"At what cost though?"

"Jackson told me you'd be perfect for the position and I agree with him. Look, talk with Cyrus; he can better explain the pros and cons of taking on a bigger role," Jameson explained.

"How long do I have before signing?"

Jameson looked at his watch and I chuckled at his response.

"You have time. Jackson doesn't want you to feel over-whelmed. Talk with your father and see what he says."

"All right, let me get out of here and get back to the office."

"I heard you have a new intern, some young girl," Jameson said, standing up to walk me out of his office.

"Yeah, Kendra hired her for me."

Jameson slapped me on the shoulder as I opened the office door and strolled toward the elevator.

"You should think about settling down, too much work will have you exhausted," Jameson said, hitting the call button for the elevator. I slid my hands in my pockets.

"Once the charity race is over, I plan on taking some time off," I told him.

"Good. Well, call me if anything changes," Jameson said just as the elevator doors closed.

\* \* \*

A few minutes later I was back at the office, sitting in the conference room with Canon, Margo, Kendra, and Asia discussing the agenda over the next few months. Margo set up a projector for us to see what the campaigns would look like if we stayed on budget and the timeline of everyone's schedule for traveling, specifically Arianna and myself.

"Kendra, I'll need you to travel with me for the press tour. Asia, you'll stay here and manage the office calls," I said.

"You don't think this would be a perfect opportunity for Asia?" Kendra questioned.

"I agree with Kendra," Asia said.

"This campaign is too important, plus the charity race is happening at the same time," I answered.

"Asia, what are you majoring in?" Canon questioned her.

"Managerial Entrepreneurship and Business studies."

"It was through All Hand Homes with Reece and Cyrus?" Canon asked. Asia nodded in answer.

"I think she can handle the travel, Malik. You know I hate flying," Kendra complained.

I chortled and shook my head.

"Fine, you win once again. Asia can come to Cyrus Premier Enterprises with me as a trial run for my meeting with Cyrus," I answered.

"Perfect!" Asia commented.

"Asia, can you grab some more coffee for us?" I asked and she jumped up to go refill the coffee pot. I waited for the door to close before I spoke.

"Kendra, I want it to be clear, that if she fucks up, I put the responsibility on you."

"Give her time, Malik, you don't like anyone new," Kendra stated as she rolled her eyes.

"I don't like anyone that's constantly eyeballing me," I remarked. Kendra scoffed and waved me off.

"You think every woman wants you," Kendra told me as the door opened and Asia walked back in before we could continue our conversation.

"Look, it's late and I'm ready to hit the road for the day. Kendra, make sure Asia has everything she needs for tomorrow." I jumped up to head out for the day. A strong glass of bourbon and a soft body to work off the long day. Reaching in my pocket for my cell phone and texted my usual on-call friend, Alyssa.

*Me: Where you at?*

*Alyssa: Hotel. Working.*

*Me: Perfect. I'll meet you there.*

*Alyssa: Anything specific you need?*

*Me: You on your knees.*

As I finished typing my response with my head down, I smelled a sweet perfume, not too heavy, more floral and lavender. I scanned the reception area and noticed Sarai talking with Jackson in front of his office. Sarai's back was to me and he motioned at me with a wave. I nodded back, heading in the opposite direction to leave for the day. I chuckled at the deep scowl on her face when she saw me, and I decided not to respond or give her the attention she wanted.

\* \* \*

"Shit." I grunted as Alyssa's mouth went up and down my thick girth. Her warm mouth drew me in, and as I closed my eyes the last person I wanted to see popped into my head.

"Sarai," I whispered.

"Who?" Alyssa screeched, plopping my dick out of her mouth.

"Shit, sorry Alyssa," I said, out of breath, moving a piece of hair behind her ear.

"You just called me another woman's name, Malik," Alyssa yelled and moved to the edge of the bed. I was dressed in only my boxers and shirt while sitting against the headboard. She worked at the hotel as manager and often was my go-to lady when I wanted company. We both knew this wasn't a relationship, but sometimes she got in her feelings.

"Alyssa, it was a mistake," I said.

Alyssa stepped out of the bed and grabbed her dress off the floor.

"What are you doing?" I questioned.

"Leaving. I can't believe you," Alyssa responded as she slipped her dress on over her head.

"So, you're pissed now?"

She shot daggers at me as she grabbed her shoes. I ran a hand down my face and shrugged, not caring to explain myself. I got out of bed and redressed to head home for the night.

"Malik, you're really going to stand here and not explain? You called me another woman's name. What if I called out another guy's name?" she questioned.

I shrugged my shoulders in answer.

"Fuck you, Malik, and you're paying for the room," Alyssa demanded. I chuckled and tried to kiss her on the cheek, and she pushed me aside.

"Charge it to my account," I said and walked off. She

continued yelling behind my back as I strolled out of the room.

"Fuck you!" Alyssa screamed.

Alyssa was a beautiful woman, but she was too attached into thinking one day I'd want her as a permanent girlfriend and wife. Something I planned on never doing and me calling out Sarai's name was an innocent mistake since I just saw her a few minutes before I showed up to meet Alyssa. Finally making it home, I opened the door as Cicely was walking out with her purse and jacket. I checked the time and it was close to eight.

"Sorry, Cicely, traffic was crazy."

I hugged and kissed her on the cheek.

"Traffic or your hotel hookup?" Cicely joked.

"Both."

"Well, I left you some food on the stove and you should get some sleep," Cicely said.

"I will, thanks."

"Long day?" she asked.

"Yeah, but I'm in for the night."

"Nice and congrats on the promotion," Cicely said, standing on the other side of the door that I held open.

"My mom can't keep shit to herself I see."

Cicely laughed and tapped me on the chest. "She just loves you and wants the best. Don't forget Sunday dinner," Cicely reminded me and I nodded, watching her step on the elevator to leave. I closed the door and stepped into the kitchen to eat and drink a glass of bourbon before I fell asleep for the night. Tomorrow, I had a meeting with Cyrus and a few calls with some reporters about the announcement.

# Chapter Three

## Malik

After a night of Alyssa texting me to apologize for overreacting, I told her we could meet up again this weekend if I didn't have any other plans. My parents usually wanted all the kids over for dinner on Sunday and tonight I planned on poker night with the fellas at my place. We usually came together to talk about our lives and women weren't allowed. I held the door open for Asia and she smiled, swishing her hips ahead of me into Cyrus's office. We drove my car instead of taking the usual town car and driver, so I could continue responding to emails and phone calls.

"Malik!" Reece called out, standing up from Cyrus's desk and coming around to hug me.

"Reece, how are you doing?" I kissed her cheek.

"I'm good and I just got off the phone with Arianna about an hour ago," Reece said.

"Is she at the track?" I questioned, shaking Cyrus's hand, and standing next to Reece while Asia took a seat.

"She was with Asia," she said to me before turning to my intern.

"Everything working out with Malik here?

"It is, thanks," Asia said.

"That's right. You two worked at Cyrus Premier Enterprises together," I said and pointed between the two.

"We haven't met, I'm Cyrus," he said, extending a hand toward Asia.

I came around his desk and took a seat next to Asia so we could get the meeting started. Reece kissed Cyrus on the lips and said goodbye. Cyrus's eyes stayed on Reece as she walked out of the room. I cleared my throat to get his attention.

"Sorry," Cyrus said.

"Did we interrupt something?" I questioned.

"Funny. Anyway, I spoke with Jackson early this week and he was on board with another charity race for Cyrus Premier Enterprises and All Hands Home," Cyrus said.

"What do Kash and Arianna say about this? I'd prefer not to see my sister end up in another crash."

A low "oh my god" came from Asia.

"That will not happen this year," Cyrus said.

"What assurances do you have in place?"

"Reece and Sarai are putting extra security in place for the day, no one will go into the garages without security, and I have Brody managing with Tripp to look at every car before they roll out to the track," Cyrus advised. Out of the corner of my eye, I saw Asia was taking notes.

"Arianna has some photoshoots coming up for the new clothing line and travel engagements."

"When were you thinking of traveling?" Cyrus asked, looking at his calendar.

Asia pulled up my calendar on her phone and passed it over to me.

"I was thinking of flying out to New York and meeting with the designers in a month."

"Maybe set the race up a month after?" Cyrus replied.

"Is that enough time for Reece and Sarai?"

"I could help," Asia commented.

"I need you to focus on the clothing line."

"Let me call Sarai and see what she thinks," Cyrus said, dialing a number on his phone.

Two rings later, a soft, elegant voice echoed through the phone.

"Hey, Cyrus," Sarai said.

"Sarai, are you free to come to my office?"

"Uhmmm...Reece ordered sushi for me," Sarai said over the phone.

"It won't take long." Cyrus stated.

"Sorry, Cyrus!" Reece shouted.

"I can come down for a few minutes, but I have to meet with Reece about the charity," Sarai insisted.

"Malik and I wanted to see what dates we can schedule the charity race for this year," Cyrus told her.

"It's normally around three months out before the premier start of the season," Sarai replied.

"This year we have a merchandising launch to plan," I interrupted.

"I have it on my list, and I was planning on talking with Jackson about it," Sarai snapped.

"He's put me in charge of it this year, so all your questions and concerns should go through me," I told her.

"When did that change?" Sarai asked.

"Since I told him it would be best for me to take it off his hands."

"Sarai, send us your ideas and who you plan on inviting for reporters," Cyrus told her.

"Sounds good. I'll email over a few ideas before our trip," Sarai stated.

"Tell Reece to make sure she answers her phone when I call in an hour," Cyrus stated and hung up.

"If Sarai is overwhelmed, I can take over managing the plans, Malik," Asia insisted.

I checked the time on my watch, thinking of the next meeting with Jackson and Arianna.

"Cyrus, we can have Asia assist Sarai at the party."

"You know they're getting ready to go out of town," Cyrus informed me.

"Who's going out of town?" I questioned, getting out of the chair.

"Reece, Arianna, Sarai, and Essence."

"Where are they going?"

"I think Mexico for a few days to have a girls' trip or something."

"At least it's not Vegas," I joked, remembering the time Arianna ended up on the front page of the gossip blogs after being spotted with Kash.

"That won't be happening this time," Cyrus chortled.

*Is Sarai dating someone?* I wondered.

"Malik, do you need me to call Kendra to have lunch delivered for you and Jackson?" Asia asked.

"I need to check on something, not right now."

"Malik, I'll see you tonight," Cyrus called out as I left his office.

"For sure and bring cash," I replied.

I left the door to his office open and headed out to the track. I figured Kamden would be here around this time doing some practice runs. I walked into the garage and saw Tripp and Kamden laughing while standing over his car.

"What's so funny? I want to laugh," I said and dapped fists with Kash and Tripp.

"What are you doing here?" Kamden, my brother-in-law, asked. To all his fans and the world he's known as Kash. When he met and married my sister, he insisted we call him by his first name, Kamden, and treat him like anyone else.

"I had a meeting with Cyrus and decided to stop off before I headed back to the office."

"Who's this?" Tripp asked, smiling at Asia.

"You better not let Essence see that smile," I taunted.

"Essence and I are friends," Tripp said.

Kamden and I peered over at Tripp and busted out in laughter.

"I want to hear you say that when I have Arianna bring her around," I said.

"Fuck no!" Tripp shouted and shook his head, wiping his hand on the towel.

"Asia, this is Kash and his pit crew team member, Tripp.Guys this is my new intern." I pointed at Asia and she stuck her hand out for a shake.

"Kash, I'm a huge fan of yours. That last race you did the other day was amazing," Asia said, holding Kash's left hand with both of her hands. Kamden politely removed his hand and stuck it in his pocket.

"What's up with you? Is Arianna all right?" Kamden asked.

"She's good, I wanted to double check to see if the both of you are still coming to poker night?" I questioned as I noticed Asia walking around the garage, taking in the equipment and information on the wall. Tripp followed behind her and explained everything.

"She's trouble," Kamden commented, motioning towards Asia.

"Not for me, because she's too young and not my type," I replied.

"Be careful anyway, her type will get you in trouble. Take it from me, the reformed bad boy who is now married," Kamden joked.

"I hear you and it's strictly a working relationship."

"We'll see, but I'll be at poker tonight. I'm not sure about Tripp or Cyrus," Kamden said.

"Cyrus is coming. Let me get her back to the office so we can wrap up the day," I told him.

"Yo, did you meet with Cyrus about the charity race for this year?" Kamden questioned.

"We just confirmed, and I have to meet with Sarai and Reece. Plus, check Arianna's schedule," I said, pulling my phone out of my pocket and checking the time.

"Sarai's going out of town on a girls' trip with Arianna in a few weeks," Kamden reminded me.

"I know, which means I need to set up a meeting asap. Let me get out of here, bro, and I'll see you later." I slapped hands with him and walked toward Tripp to confirm tonight.

An hour later, I was wrapping up things at the office and finishing a phone call with the head of maintenance for Pierce Motors to make sure things were running smoothly at the track from facilities, to building touch ups, to events. This reminded me I needed to schedule a sit down with Sarai before she left for her trip. A knock on the door prompted me to finish my call with Gregory otherwise he'd have me on the phone all day.

"Gregory, let me call you back," I said and hung up, then called out for whoever was on the other side of the door to come in.

"Hey, I wanted to check and see if you needed anything before I leave," Asia said, walking up to the side of my desk.

"Is Kendra still here?" I questioned.

"Nope, just little old me," Asia answered and tried to sit on the edge of my desk.

"Then you're free to go," I told her.

Asia bit down on the pen in her mouth. "Are you sure? I mean I can do some filing or type up your schedule," Asia said, sliding her hand across my desk and patting the top of my palm.

"Positive, you can go, Asia."

"Yes," she said, standing up straight.

"I'm not interested, and I expect you to be professional at all times."

"Oh...I'm sorry if I come across as overzealous. I'm a touchy person with everyone," Asia commented, smiling at me.

"I've noticed, just want to be clear so we don't have any misunderstandings in the future."

"Asia, are you ready to go?" A soft, but stern voice at the door questioned. I peered around Asia and Sarai was standing there in a dark pants suit that melded to her curves. Her hair was pulled back into a ponytail and she was wearing light makeup as well as a hard glare on her face. I didn't know what her problem was and had no time to find out. I chuckled to myself. Asia stepped closer to my desk. "Hey, Sarai, I'm ready. Let me wrap up with Malik."

"Mr. Pierce...you mean," Sarai informed her as she stood with her arms crossed over her chest.

Asia looked over her shoulder. "Yes, Mr. Pierce...Uhm do you need anything else?"

"No, but I need to talk with Sarai," I replied.

"I can stay and take notes," Asia answered as she batted her lashes.

"No, alone," I replied.

She glanced between me and Sarai. The tension in the room was heavy, which was strange to me because they were family, and I had no interest in either woman. Yes, Sarai was beautiful, sexy, and worked hard in her career. But she was too stubborn and thought she knew everything and was unwilling to listen.

"Okay, sure. I'll wait for you at my desk, Sarai," Asia told her.

Sarai nodded and stepped into my office. I stood up and walked toward the door, closing it, and strolling to the front of my desk.

"Are you managing the charity race this year?" I questioned.

"Yes, like I do every year."

"Cut the attitude, Sarai."

"I don't have an attitude, Mr. Pierce. Is there something you need at this moment?"

"I need you and Reece to get the final details of the charity race to me on my desk in two weeks."

"That's not possible."

"Why not?"

"We're going out of town and then I have an event for

Kamden and Cyrus Premier Enterprises to plan," Sarai told me.

"Maybe we should get someone else to manage our publicity department if you're too busy."

Sarai chortled. "I'm not, you can email me your suggestions and I'll connect with Reece."

"I want to make sure what happened to Arianna doesn't happen again this year," I said.

Her eyes bored into me. "I agree, Mr. Pierce, and that's why I'll personally oversee everything with Reece."

"Then we agree that we will need to work alongside each other to check backgrounds, interview staff, and keep security tight at all times. My sister won't be subjected to any harassment like last time," I announced.

"We do. Reece and I can meet with you when we get back," Sarai said and stomped out of my office.

* * *

Jay Z was blasting from the speaker as Cicely prepared all my favorites, including hot wings, sliders, Philly cheesesteaks, fries, spinach dip, egg rolls, and chocolate cake. I picked up beer, Hennessey, scotch, and Ciroc. Cyrus, Kamden, Tripp, Canon, and Jackson sat around my dining room table while SportsCenter played the latest basketball game. We joked and drank while playing poker.

"Tripp, you have no clue what you're doing," Cyrus glared, and his nostrils flared.

"Who invited you again?" Jackson asked and I almost spit my beer out when Tripp held both hands up pointing at himself.

"That's cold, Jackson," I said.

"No what's cold is Tripp losing all his money," Jackson joked.

"Where's EJ at?" Canon questioned.

"He had to watch the kids tonight because Gabriella went out to dinner with the girls."

"Yeah, Reece cut plans short so she could hang with them," Cyrus complained.

"You sound like this guy," I said and pointed at Kamden.

"What? I can't help that I love my wife and would rather be with her than you guys," Kamden replied, eating hot wings.

"We're not here to talk about being in love and shit," I announced as I placed a royal flush down on the table.

Canon and Cyrus each had two pair and Jackson a three of a kind.

"Aren't you seeing that girl from the hotel?" Jackson questioned and I shook my head no. Jackson smoked on the Cuban cigars I had ordered and dealt the next hand.

"She's fun, but nothing serious," I answered as I poured another shot of scotch.

"She must have wanted a relationship," Kamden taunted.

"That part," Canon joked.

"Man, I'm telling you, women are crazy. They think just because a guy sleeps with you a few times, it means I'm ready to become committed or something," I ranted.

"Depends on what expectations you made in the beginning," Cyrus stated.

"What did you tell Reece?" I asked.

"In the beginning, I wasn't looking for anything serious. Over time, though, my views changed and I couldn't see myself without her," Cyrus explained.

"Alyssa was overdramatic and more interested in becoming someone's wife."

"Jackson, didn't you sleep with Emery the first day and marry her like a week later?" Tripp asked.

"No, but she was mine after that night though," Jackson told him, and everybody burst in laughter at his statement.

"Take it from me, Malik, bachelorhood gets old fast," Cyrus said, taking a wing off Kamden's plate.

"Get your own food," Kamden complained.

We laughed as Cyrus stole another wing off Kamden's plate. Canon picked up the box of cigars, passed one toward me and we smoked alongside Jackson and talked for the rest of the night.

# Chapter Four

## Sarai

I was out to dinner with Reece, Gabriella, and Arianna. Emery wasn't feeling well so she stayed home. Gabriella picked over her ravioli, Arianna and I ordered the salmon and brown rice, and Reece was eating asparagus and baked chicken. The waiter refilled my glass of wine as Reece explained the hotel for our upcoming girls' trip to the Bahamas.

"We have the two suites connected with a large balcony," Reece said.

"I can't wait to get away," I spoke.

"Me too. Running a practice, and dealing with kids and a husband is draining," Gabriella said.

"Sarai, did you talk with Malik about doing the publicity work for the charity race?" Arianna asked.

I rolled my eyes at the mention of his name. Taking another sip of my red wine, I closed my eyes taking in the crisp, clean, sweet taste. I opened my eyes back up and all the girls were staring at me.

"What?"

"Cyrus told me we needed to set up a meeting with him to discuss the dinner and race," Reece stated.

"Don't remind me," I mumbled under my breath.

"What did Malik do this time? I know my brother can be overbearing and want to control everything," Arianna said before she wiped the napkin across her lips.

My night was going well until she brought him up at the dinner table. Malik Pierce was my client and best friend's older brother. I had my own publicity firm and represented celebrities, athletes, and corporations. For example, I worked with All Hands Home, Kamden, and Cyrus Premier Enterprises. You wouldn't find anyone in California that wasn't represented by my firm, Lambert Publicity, and my skills could turn anyone into a star. My family was still surprised by how much attention my name brought in the news or social media by the work we did. At twenty-eight and a boss in my own right, I was smart, funny, and a little cocky with a heart of gold. Also, I was learning to get over heartbreak like any other woman because I let someone have my entire space and mindset and they took it and ran it into the ground. Often people think I should have gone into modeling or acting because of my slim figure with curves and my height of five-eight with plump lips, high cheekbones, full breasts, and wide hips like my mother, DeeDee. So many times, I heard her complaining to my aunts about me needing to learn how to forgive and go back to my ex-boyfriend, Christopher, a high-profile actor who cheated on me with another actress in the business. They became the new *Brangelina* in the industry and the talk of the town. Everywhere I went for an event, somehow one of them would show up, and I'd get the questions of 'how do you feel?' since the situation was still an open wound. Eight months later, Christopher was still trying to get back with me even though I knew he was still seeing the girl that he cheated on me with and pretending it was a one-time thing.

"He wants to control the charity race plans," I responded.

"Malik is the VP, so his name is on the line if things fall apart," Reece explained.

"My name is on the line too with my business. It's mostly that he's worried about something happening like last year."

"He can't control everything," Arianna informed me.

"Tell him that," I told her.

"Malik probably still has guilt from not being able to fix it before you got hurt," Gabriella explained. I became close friends with Gabriella through Eddison Jr. when he recommended I go see her about representing her business as one of my early clients and we became best friends. Him being the oldest and Arianna the youngest, he treated me like a little sister, while Malik pushed my buttons every time we ended up in the same room. It was always a challenge or a game for him to go against any opinion I brought up.

"Is he dating anyone?" Reece asked.

"He's probably got a gang of women on speed dial, just like the rest of these vain, self-centered men," I spoke while cutting a piece of the salmon. All eyes stared at me. "What?"

"You like him," Arianna excitedly screeched.

"What! Ari calm down. No one likes your brother," I stated.

"When's the last time you had a date?" Gabriella questioned.

"Over seven months ago, when I broke up with Christopher," I said.

"Malik isn't all that bad," Arianna replied.

"I could see you two together," Reece said, tasting a piece of food off my plate.

"Unsee it please. I'd rather not have to end up with another over-arrogant jackass.".

"Ari and Kash started out unconventional, maybe you and Malik could do the same thing," Reece mused.

"How is everything with you and Cyrus?" I asked.

"Nice try changing the subject," Reece answered.

"This is the last time I do girls' night. All of my friends have husbands and boyfriends now."

"You could be like us if you gave love another try," Ari spoke up. I shook my head no.

"Love doesn't work for me anymore."

"Why? Because you have to be vulnerable and open with your emotions?" Reece asked.

"Preach," Gabriella said.

"She doesn't want to come across as weak and needing someone," Ari stated, pointing out one of my insecurities that I tried to keep hidden. After the too many chances I gave to Chris, I thought I wasn't good enough because he kept finding ways to take advantage of my love.

"This salmon is really good," I said.

"You're good at your job, Sarai, but you never take the time to focus on yourself the way you should," Reece said.

"I'm going on the girls' trip with you, so my self-care starts then."

"Yeah, but what happens when you get back into town and around your cousins and family members?" Ari asked.

"What's wrong with her family?" Gabriella questioned.

"How much time do you have?" Ari retorted.

"My family's not that bad," I said.

"Sarai, you're the strongest, most headstrong person I've ever met, but when you get around your family, something in you becomes too eager to please them," Ari stated.

"When did this turn into the Sarai therapy session?" I grunted.

"We only want you to be happy, Sarai," Reece said.

"Let's change the subject please," I insisted.

"The fixer that needs fixing," Ari muttered.

I flipped her off and continued eating my food and ignored their conversations on dating. I didn't need to be reminded of my past and mistakes, or how my family wasn't the most supportive of my choices in men.

Forty minutes later I was getting out of the cab in front of my condo and stepping inside the elevator gripping my keys. It had just turned midnight and I was exhausted from the day. After being on my feet all day and then having dinner, I was tempted to take off my shoes here. But the elevator dinged first, and I stepped off on the penthouse floor. This was the same building Kamden used to live in and he actually sold me his place for a lower cost. I wasn't ready to buy a home since I traveled so much. Strolling out, I bumped into a brick wall of a hard-chiseled body wearing only a white t-shirt and gray jogging sweatpants.

"What are you doing here so late?" Malik asked.

I checked my watch, seeing it showed going one a.m.

"It's late and I live here," I quipped as I motioned toward Kamden's old place.

"Since when?" Malik wondered, holding a trash bag and staring at me. I pulled on my dress, feeling his eyes on me.

"Since Kamden sold it to me a few weeks ago," I answered, not wanting to explain that I left my old place that I shared with Christopher and stayed with my mom, then eventually got tired of being under constant scrutiny.

"You have fun with your friends?" Malik asked.

I walked around him and inserted my key in the door. "Not that it's any of your business, but I did."

He chuckled. "That mouth, Sarai, is terrible."

"I get that a lot," I told him, walking inside of my place and shutting the door in his face.

I leaned against the door and blew out an exasperated breath and closed my eyes, cursing myself out for having that last glass of wine at dinner. For a moment, I actually thought Malik was attractive outside of his usual suits.

I pulled off my shoes and headed to my bedroom where I removed my dress, tossed it over the couch, and grabbed my silk robe. I couldn't sleep without taking my makeup off at night, so I picked up a makeup wipe remover and cleaned my face when the doorbell rang.

"Who the hell is that?" I asked myself before sliding my feet into my black kitty house shoes. I looked through the peephole and sighed. Turning the knob, I opened the door and Malik's eyes and mouth focused on my body in the robe. I cleared my throat. "Yeah?"

"You left this in the Uber. The doorman gave it to me when he saw me in the mailroom," Malik said, holding out my purse.

"Thanks," I replied, grabbing it from him, forgetting I took out my keys from my bag.

"I figure since you're living in Kamden's place now, Cicely works for you," Malik said.

I nodded. "Basically, I inherited her from Kamden. She refused to cut her hours down," I joked.

"That's Cicely," Malik replied.

There was an awkward silence between us.

"Uhm. Well, I need to get some sleep for tomorrow. Because someone is demanding I meet with them," I hinted. He chortled and stepped back, heading toward his apartment. I closed the door, leaned against it, and closed my eyes.

"You can't, Sarai. He's off-limits," I said to myself. Heading back to my bedroom I finished cleaning off my makeup, brushed my teeth, and got in bed to sleep the rest of the night away. Right as I closed my eyes and set the alarm, my phone buzzed, and I picked it up off the charger on the nightstand.

*Christopher: I know it's late but I miss you.*

*Me: I don't care.*

*Christopher: You answered this message, which means you care.*

I shook my head before I sent another message back. I refused to feed into his ego, so I deleted the conversation out of my phone and closed out of messages, then rolled over and went to sleep.

# Chapter Five

## Sarai

After oversleeping it was past nine a.m. and I was rushing out of the condo to avoid being late and missing Cicely's famous blueberry pancakes. I made it to Cyrus Premier Enterprises to meet with Reece about the charity race. I smiled at Thomas as he walked out of her office and I walked inside.

"You look cute," Reece said. I looked down at my navy blue pants suit with a large black wraparound belt and animal print heels.

"I don't feel cute," I replied, placing my black binder with all my notes and contacts down.

"What's going on with you?" Reece questioned, offering me a cup of coffee.

"I had one already and I didn't get much sleep."

"Why not?" Reece asked.

"Well, it started with me bumping into Malik after I left dinner with you guys. Then Christopher texted me," I complained.

"Wait, Malik didn't know you lived in Kamden's old place?" Reece asked.

"No, and I preferred not having him as a neighbor."

"Malik's not that bad," Reece said.

I didn't want to admit that one of the reasons I couldn't sleep was because of my dreams about Malik and me in bed together. Doing things that we shouldn't be doing. He wasn't my type and the complete opposite of me.

"You're friends with him so of course you'll stick up for him."

"I met him through Arianna and Cyrus's business dealings with his family," Reece explained.

"Well, I want to keep things professional. So, the first thing on the agenda is planning a theme for the charity dinner after the race," I said.

Reece turned toward her computer and typed something up and turned the computer toward me. "Last year you know we did an auction date type of thing, but it didn't happen because of Arianna's accident," Reece said.

"Are you thinking of doing it again?" I questioned.

"We should do a silent auction, no dates. If people want to donate a date with a celebrity, we can."

"But keep it a silent auction, maybe have some art pieces, movie premiere tickets so I can pull some things together with my contacts."

"That's a good idea."

"I could talk with Jackson and see what they can offer from Pierce Motors."

"I know Cyrus will donate from Cyrus Premier Enterprises," Reece insisted.

As she talked, I took down more notes.

"What about the girls' trip?" Reece asked.

"I can't wait to get on a beach and lay out with a mojito," I told her.

"Cyrus is giving us the private jet and if we want to do something else, we can. Maybe Vegas?" Reece hinted.

I shook my head no.

"I remember the last time you guys did Vegas. I had to figure out a way to get Kamden out of the mess he made with Arianna."

Reece giggled. "Believe me, I was just as surprised as anyone else."

"Those two drove me crazy."

"Just imagine what I went through with Cyrus. You had a small taste of public backlash with them," Reece stated.

"You're right, and that reminds me I need to send Cyrus the mockup logo sketches for Cyrus Premier Enterprises."

"Thomas wants the company and All Hands Home charity to be promoted on the sign of the step and repeat," Reece said.

"I was planning that already and even planned to send out invitations with both names," I replied.

"Amazing. What are you doing tonight?"

"Dinner with my mom and then home."

"If you're not out late, Arianna wants to go to the club."

"Let me think about it, Reece. I'd hate to run into any of Christopher's friends."

"His friends act like him." Reece stated.

"My mom wants me to take him back."

"Listen, I'm the last person to tell you what you should do. But Christopher is not good for you, Sarai."

"I know and I told him to go fuck off. So, I'll see if he takes the hint," I said, closing my folder.

"Where are you headed to now?" Reece wondered, standing up and following behind me to the door.

"I need to run over to a photoshoot to check on Arianna and then check in with Cyrus and Jackson," I said.

"Okay, keep me updated if you're down," Reece said.

"I will! Talk later, bestie," I said and hugged her goodbye. Once I was out of the building, I jumped in my car and drove to Long Beach to Dagger Studios. I hit the Bluetooth on my car and dialed Cyrus's number.

"Hello," Cyrus said.

"Hey, Cyrus, this is Sarai."

"Sarai, how are you?" he questioned.

"I'm good. I finished up a meeting with Reece and I wanted to send over the mockup logo."

"Perfect! So, things are looking good for the charity race?" Cyrus asked.

"Yes. I know Malik wanted an update. I'm headed to the photoshoot with Arianna right now."

"Great. Did you and Reece get the guest list together?" Cyrus questioned as I heard typing over the phone. I signaled to get over on the freeway as I took the exit to get off toward the side street to Dagger Studios.

"It's more intimate this time with under two hundred people."

"Sounds good to me," Cyrus said.

"Me too. Thanks again, Cyrus. I'll have my assistant send it over to you before the end of the day." He said goodbye and I hung up, turned into the studio, then parked in the open spot for employees. I do a lot of work with Dagger Studios with my clients and corporate events. I grabbed my shades and purse and turned the car off before I stepped out and closed the door. Then I headed to the building and opened the door, feeling the cool breeze of the air conditioner and hearing Kendrick Lamar playing in the background.

"Hi, Sarai, they're in the back," Rose, the receptionist at the front desk, said.

"Thanks, Rose."

I walked around the desk in the lobby and opened the door for the employee-only entrance and saw Arianna standing in front of the white background with the flashes of a camera clicking in front of her face. She was posing in different positions and smiling. I scanned the room and saw Malik and my cousin, Asia. At first, I was annoyed when Asia wanted to come here to work as an intern. She had a habit of quitting after a few months and I'd prefer to not have my name run through the mud. I knew my family was pissed when I let her go at my publicity firm. Every other day she was messing up dates and times, flirting with the men. I got tired of having to pick up the slack, so I was happy things worked out at Cyrus Premier Enterprises. Now she was working as Malik's assistant. I didn't know if he was into her the way she was clinging to every word he said. She was over the top trying to flirt with him and Canon. Plus, she was doing the same thing in his office when I went to pick her up. Malik was much older than her and he seemed like he needed a woman who was on his level.

"Sarai, what are you doing here?" Asia questioned as her smile faded. David, the photographer, said to take a break.

Arianna was handed a robe to put on and she walked over toward us. She pulled me into a hug, and I bumped her in the side. "You look cute."

"I love this outfit, Sarai," Ari said as she tugged on my belt.

"Thanks, boo. I wanted to come and check up on things," I said, ignoring Asia's comment.

Malik stood with Canon as they talked with David about the photos.

"So far everything is great. Malik wanted to get started before the trip so they could do some small social media leaks," Ari stated.

"Yeah, he has me in charge of getting the hashtags and picking the bloggers," Asia mentioned. It was like she felt we were in competition together and that was not what I was about at all. I've always supported my friends' and family's dreams.

"I'm happy for you, Asia. How are things going with Malik?" I asked and pointed at him and Canon.

"Great, I'm taking on a lot more responsibility from Kendra. Plus... he asked me out." Asia leaned in close and whispered the last part.

"Who asked you out?" Arianna asked.

She bit her lip. "Your brother."

"Wow! How old are you, Asia?" Arianna asked.

"Too young," I said before I strolled over to Malik and Canon.

"Hey, Sarai," Canon said, smiling.

"Hi, gentlemen. I wanted to check and see how everything was going before I headed out for my trip this week."

"Sarai, you know I have everything on track. When are you going to take me up on the dinner offer?" David asked in front of Canon and Malik. I waved him off, because he knew I turned him down every time he asked me. I didn't like getting mixed up with people I worked with after the Christopher situation and David tried hard to break me out of my habit because he was sexy and charming. But working around women ninety percent of the time I could be honest and say I was the jealous type.

"David, you know that's not happening," I replied.

"You two dating?" Malik questioned David like I wasn't standing there.

"No, and I should ask you if you're dating my cousin. She's a little young for you, don't you think?" I spat.

His forehead furrowed. "Who told you that?" Malik asked.

"She did," I said.

"Asia? You went out with Asia's ass?" Canon asked him.

"Hell no. She asked me out and I told her I don't date anybody I work with," Malik told him.

"Well, I don't care who you date, I just came to inform you that Reece and I will have the guest list and details of the auction sent over while we're gone," I said. Asia walked over to me standing with Canon and David.

"Did I miss anything?" Asia questioned.

"Yeah, did you tell Sarai we were dating?" Malik demanded.

Her jaw clenched. "Of course not. She must have misunderstood what I said. Sarai does that a lot."

"I didn't—" I was interrupted by Arianna pulling me from the group.

"Sarai, come look at the photos really quick and let me know your thoughts," Arianna stated. My eyes followed her gaze toward the TV, scanning the images, trying to hold my temper inside before I blew up on Asia.

"What's up with your cousin?" Arianna inquired.

"Who knows. I'm trying to stay calm, but she's pissing me off with this little innocent crap," I spat.

Before Arianna could talk, my phone rang and I saw Cicely's name across the screen.

"Hi, Cicely," I answered.

"Sarai, are you still going to your mom's for dinner?" Cicely inquired.

I checked my watch to see if it wasn't too late for me to get across town and back home so I could pack.

"I am for a few minutes," I replied.

"I wanted to double check. I was planning Malik's dinner and I was checking to see if I needed to make enough for you too."

At the mention of Malik, I glanced over at him talking with Asia in the corner. It looked like he was fussing at her, because she held her head down and he was pointing at himself.

"Uhmmm...don't worry about leaving anything for me," I said and ended the call.

"Cicely needs to retire," Arianna spoke up.

"I agree, but she refuses. Which picture are they going with?" I questioned.

"Jackson wants to start with a Pierce Motors suit with the logo and fade into the shorts and workout gear," Arianna stated.

"I agree, it shows how a woman can start from her job and fade into many other roles in life," I said.

"Cool, Kamden almost freaked out at the two-piece swimsuit," Arianna commented.

I chuckled because we all knew how possessive Kash could be. He treated me like an older sister and drove me crazy back in the day when he was single. Now that he was married and a father you only saw him at family functions or with Arianna at events. Never out with his single friends anymore.

"I wouldn't expect anything less from him."

"Ari, are you ready to finish the rest of the shoot? I have a few things I need to wrap up at the office," Malik asked as he interrupted our conversation.

"Yeah. Sarai, are you staying?" Arianna asked, and I shook my head no.

"I have a prior engagement with my family, so I need to wrap up some work at my main office," I said.

"Okay, call me later so we can talk about our outfits for the trip," Arianna said and walked off.

Malik ran a hand down his face, looking over his shoulder at Asia as she stared at us.

"Your cousin lied. I'm not dating her or anybody else," Malik informed me and even though I didn't care, I felt a little relief.

"Okay... you don't owe me anything."

"You can let the armor down, Sarai," Malik told me.

"Whatever, Malik."

"Send me the information and hit me up tomorrow," Malik suggested.

I started to say something back when Asia stormed over to me.

"Sarai, you didn't have to embarrass me like that," Asia spat.

"What are you talking about?" I asked, heading outside.

"You told Malik what I said."

"Listen, Asia, your focus should be on your work and not a man."

"You should take your own advice," Asia mumbled, and I stopped to glare at her.

"What does that mean exactly?"

"It means you're once again trying to take the spotlight and fuck up my chances," Asia announced.

"Your chance at Malik?" I questioned.

"Yes! Among other things," Asia confessed as a muscle in her jaw twitched.

"I'm heading to go work at *my* company. A place *I* own and didn't need a man handing it to me or lying to get to the top," I spat.

"We both know Christopher is the reason you have your little company," Asia insisted.

"Asia, don't get your feelings hurt."

"Without Christopher you wouldn't be where you are right now," Asia said.

I tossed my purse and shades inside my car then dropped down in the seat and inserted the keys.

"If that's how you feel, cousin. You're welcome to believe that, but just remember who supported you when everyone else left you alone."

A flush crept up her face as I pulled out of the parking space and drove off into traffic, watching her stomp back inside.

# Chapter Six

## Sarai

After stopping to grab something to eat I was inside of my publicity boutique forty minutes later. I normally worked out of Cyrus Premier Enterprises. But I still had a small office for my main clients with other publicists under me that managed some of my accounts. Selena Johnson, my receptionist, and assistant, was talking on the phone and smiling when I came inside. She held up a finger for me to wait.

"That'll be fine, she just walked in now. Thanks, goodbye," Selena said and ended the call.

Selena stood up and followed me toward my office.

"How are things around here?" I asked as I kicked off my shoes and picked up my messages off my desk.

"Things are pretty quiet. No complaints from clients. They know how your schedule is around this time when Cyrus Premier Enterprises starts up," Selena told me.

"Did you get my email about the guest list from Reece?" I askedSelena stood up from the chair and walked back to pick up her iPad as I trailed her and we came back inside.

"Yes, and I went over everything before forwarding it to Cyrus," Selena explained.

"Make sure Cyrus has a table specifically for him and the team."

"Sounds good. What about Pierce Motors?"

I took a seat in my chair and shut my computer down as my phone vibrated with a message from an unknown number.

"God, I am so tired of him." I mumbled, rubbing my forehead.

"Who is it? Please don't tell me it's Christopher," Selena questioned. I lifted my phone to show her the texts.

"Yep, trying to get back in my life." I blew out a breath.

"Christopher is very bold, because he's tried to get in with a few people here a few times."

"He came here?" I asked.

"Yep, thinking he ran things and wanting to know where you were."

"Ugh... he's been texting me wanting to talk and I keep blocking him."

"He acts like we don't see him at movie premieres with his girlfriend."

"I know, and I refuse to go backwards. You know my trip is coming up, so I need you to hold things down."

"Already taken care of, the charity race is locked in, invitations sent out," Selena told me.

"Arianna's campaign is about to start, and I just left the photoshoot."

"I bet she looks amazing."

"Yep, pregnant and pretty as usual."

"I know Kash is ready for her to retire," Selena stated.

"She hasn't really been driving as much."

"Oh, I forgot to tell you that Malik wanted to talk with you about setting up an event for Pierce Motors," Selena said.

"What type of event? My schedule is full."

"He's thinking later on this year to help celebrate the position and where the team is, basically a company party," Selena explained.

"Put it on my schedule as a maybe. Priority is Cyrus Premier Enterprises and All Hand Homes."

"Sounds good."

"I won't be here too much longer. I have to head to my mom's for dinner," I groaned, grabbing my phone to call Reece.

"Tell Mommy I said hello," Selena said and stood up to leave.

"You know, DeeDee wants you to come for a visit," I said, and she waved me off. I chortled because my mom was always trying to run somebody's life.

"This better be good," Reece said.

"Why do you sound out of breath?" I joked.

"I was carrying in groceries to All Hands Home," Reece told me.

"Tell the boys I said hello."

"Kids, Sarai says hi," Reece announced over the phone.

"Hi, Sarai!" I heard the boys yell and I laughed at them. Whenever I got any spare time, I liked to go hang out or bring them around my office so they could see where I worked. I also enjoyed giving them different experiences at movie premieres.

"Oh, I'm tired," Reece said.

"You sound like it."

"I can't wait for our trip. I need to get away for a little while."

"I won't hold you up, but I was calling to let you know I'll meet you guys at the club tonight," I said.

"Really, I thought we'd have to beg you to come out," Reece joked.

She wasn't lying, because after having to set up my clients at events all day or club appearances I was over the club scene, and I wasn't in my early twenties anymore.

"Well after I had a little run in with Asia today it just reminded me that I need to live a little."

"What did she say?" Reece questioned.

"She said Malik asked her out on a date," I said as I rolled my eyes.

"Interesting," Reece said.

Selena walked into my office and handed me a file folder. I grabbed it from her and opened the file to see blogs preparing to run stories on a few of my clients and Christopher supposedly doing an interview with *Life* magazine.

"I can't stand him," I blurted out and closed the file.

"What happened?" Reece asked.

"Just work stuff. I need to send a few things out to some bloggers and contact *Life* magazine."

"Well don't stress too much and I'll see you later," Reece told me and hung up the phone.

I opened up the file folder again and looked at the lies about Arianna and Kash saying they had an open marriage. Another gossip blogger was running a story on Christopher's girlfriend saying I was trying to get him back. I typed up my response and sent off a cease and desist letter to both bloggers. I dialed an old friend at *Life* magazine to make sure whatever Christopher talked about didn't involve me. Two hours later, I left and drove straight to my mom's house for dinner. It was going on five-thirty and traffic was held up because of an accident. I parked in front of her house and turned off my car, seeing my aunt and cousin's cars out front. I sighed, preparing myself to deal with any snappy response they would try to pull on me. I got out of the car and walked up to her door and slid my key inside, hearing the loud laughter coming from the dining room. I kicked off my shoes and left them at the door along with my purse and walked down the hallway. My mother's house in Calabasas was in a nice neighborhood.

"What's for dinner?" I asked, looking around at my Aunt Gladys, my cousins, Asia and Porsha, and my mom's neighbor, Daphne.

"Hey, baby," Aunt Gladys said as she stood up to give me a hug. Porsha, my cousin and daughter of Gladys, stood up to give me a hug as well.

"Aunt DeeDee made the works and I'm starving," Porsha mentioned.

"Asia, you can't speak?" I teased. She rolled her eyes and Aunt Gladys looked between the two of us.

"What's wrong with you?" Aunt Gladys asked her.

"Nothing," Asia said then jumped up and headed to the kitchen.

I picked up the wineglass from Porsha's hand and took a sip and sat down on the couch. I looked around the room and noticed my mother had redecorated a few things since the last time I was here. The living room colors were black and cream with a fireplace installed, a chandelier was mounted up top, and a few paintings hung around the walls next to the family photos.

"She's been pissy ever since she came here," Porsha announced.

"You two fighting?" Aunt Gladys asked.

"Not that I know of, but you know Asia is always doing something."

"Finally, you got here," my mother, DeeDee, said, walking into the room.

"Sorry, traffic was crazy."

"Well, you're here now, come eat. I just set everything up," Mom told me.

"Asia said you're trying to take her man, Malik," Porsha mumbled to me.

"I'm not dealing with her," I spat and walked into the kitchen and sat down on the chair across from Asia. The table was filled with egg rolls, fried fish, steamed corn, green beans, and orange chicken.

"Asia says you're trying to steal her boyfriend, Sarai," Mom blurted out and I almost choked on my food. My aunt patted my back to help me and I took a sip of the water to clear my throat.

"What man?" I inquired, cutting into my fish.

"Malik, her boss," Mom said.

"When did he become your man, Asia?"

"You two are dating right?" Mom peered at Asia.

The table got quiet as Asia squirmed in her seat.

"It's still early, Auntie," Asia told her.

"Malik is not dating Asia. I'm not dating him either."

"Your continued involvement in our business is the reason for that," Asia snapped as she slammed her hand on the table.

"Asia, lower your voice when you talk to me," I said and pointed my fork at her.

"Sarai, get off your high horse. Malik and I have

talked, and he might have told you we weren't together to keep you out of our business," Asia explained.

I nodded because she could be telling the truth, but I don't care to listen anymore.

"Well have fun with him," I said.

"What's wrong with you, Sarai? Lately you've been snippy," Mom said. Here she was bringing up side comments to make false narratives of me miserable.

"Mom, you haven't seen me in over two weeks. Don't start up again."

"So, you're saying you've purposely stayed away from me," Mom said and wiped her mouth with a napkin.

"I've been busy with work and every chance I do get to come here you start up again about Christopher."

"Sorry if I think you made a mistake," Mom explained.

"The man cheated and still tried to bash me in public and on social media," I said, getting frustrated by her always sticking up for other people more than me.

"Maybe you should have paid him more attention," Asia muttered.

"Asia, if you want to walk out of here tonight instead of leaving on a stretcher, I suggest you shut up."

"Girl, please," Asia mumbled and motioned me off.

"You two need to calm down, Sarai. Yes, Christopher made a mistake, but he apologized and went to therapy to get help," Mom said, trying to get me to feel bad for him. The only reason she was speaking nice about him was because she thought being with Christopher would bring more status and money to herself.

"Asia, how is your job going?" Aunt Gladys questioned.

"Things are going well. I might be getting promoted soon," Asia said.

"Huh."

"Sarai, stop it," Mom scolded me.

"Look at the time, I need to go and meet with Reece." I jumped up, not finishing my food. I bent down and kissed my aunt and cousin on the cheek. I marched out of the kitchen to the living room and slid my shoes on. Mom came into the living room with her arms crossed.

I picked up my keys and purse.

"I don't want to hear it, Mom."

"I'm not going to argue with you, Sarai. When I hear things from your cousin, I get worried," Mom said.

"Why are you listening to her over me?"

"She comes around," Mom spat.

"Because she's always wanting something, and you give it to her."

"Okay, Asia can be a little overdramatic. What about Christopher?" Mom asked.

I rubbed my temples. "You want me to be like you and stay with someone that doesn't really love me and I refuse to do that."

"Your father made mistakes. I can admit I wasn't protective enough of him coming in and out of your life," Mom said.

"Mom let's talk about this another time. When you have less company over," I stated, then I leaned over and kissed her cheek, opened the front door, and walked out.

Asia was working my last nerve and before I kicked her ass in my mom's house, I needed to leave and have a drink. I jumped in my car and drove off, heading home to change before meeting Reece for drinks.

\* \* \*

Thirty minutes later, after washing up and changing, I put on a light blue bodycon dress and my Sophie Winston heels, leaving my hair down.

Heather and Reece waved me over to their section and I saw Essence and Arianna with them. I walked through the crowd as men tried to talk to me and pull me toward the dance floor. Shaking my head, I motioned to my group of friends in VIP and made it to them before the crowd got bigger.

"You made it!" Reece cheered and stood up to hug me.

"I needed a stiff drink to relax after my day," I replied, bending down to hug Heather, Essence, and Arianna.

"What are you drinking?" I questioned.

"Lemon drop martini," Essence said, dancing in her seat.

"How long have you guys been here?" I asked.

"Heather had a client event tonight so she was here an hour before us," Reece shouted over the loud music.

"So free drinks tonight!" I excitedly said.

"How are things in your publicist world?" Heather asked. We were in the same position, representing brands and clients in the public eye, so she could understand how things changed constantly with keeping your name in a positive light.

I sat down between Arianna and Essence and leaned over to talk to Heather.

"Busy! I'm ready for this girls trip though."

Heather nodded. "Same. I told Reece I wish I could go with you guys, but I have a big event at the same time," Heather reminded me.

"We'll have plenty more trips," Reece stated.

"Did Cyrus freak out when you left the house in this?" I commented, motioning up and down at her short black dress with the back out.

"He was fine. I just needed to make sure he was happy when I left," Reece teased and winked her left eye. All of us burst into laughter knowing how it was when you had a significant other who could be a little jealous and possessive.

"Essence, what's going on with you lately?" I inquired.

"Nothing much, just working," Essence said as she took a sip of her drink.

"Yeah, working Tripp's last nerves," Arianna taunted, poking Essence in the shoulder.

"Are you dating Tripp for real?" I asked.

Essence rolled her eyes at Arianna. "I'm single and we're friends."

"She's getting the big D!" All of them screamed at the same time and laughed.

"What about you?" Essence questioned.

"I'm single and plan on keeping it that way," I said.

"That won't last with the way these men are looking at you in here," Arianna said. I waved off the lingering looks from the men in the room and continued talking with the girls. A waitress came over and dropped two bottles of Ciroc and a bottle of Atlas down on the table.

"Let's celebrate us being the best in everything we do and being supportive of each other," Reece said.

"I agree," I said and picked up a glass to pour a little champagne.

Arianna stood up and started dancing with Essence in front of the section looking down on the crowd. Feeling the vibe of the drink I got up and join them.

"All right, Sarai! I see you, boo." Reece grinned, cheering me on. I swayed my hips to the side and twerked a little even though the dress cut off a little circulation. It fit my body perfectly and showed off every curve.

"Come on, Reece! Cyrus can't stop you tonight," I coached her to get up and join. Heather had to go check on her client. Reece stood up and came around to the balcony section next to us and all four of us started dancing side by side to the latest Cardi B song. All eyes were on the four of us as the lights focused on our little section. Rarely was I the center of attention but today was the exception since I was feeling so good. As I continued dancing, strong hands wrapped around my waist and a kiss grazed the back of my neck.

"You're sexy in this dress, baby," Christopher said in my ear, and I froze. Pushing him away, I jerked back when he tried to grab my hand.

"What the hell are you doing?" I yelled.

"Baby, come on. It's me. Let me talk to you really quick," Christopher said and reached out to grab my hand again.

"How did you get in here?" I questioned, looked around for security.

"Sarai, it's me. You can't keep me out of anything," Christopher told me.

I could feel my buzz waning. Arianna stood in front of me as protection, but I didn't want her getting involved and causing her brothers to come out here and make it a bigger issue. Stepping around her, I pointed for Christopher to follow me out of the section toward the hallway to talk in private. I told the girls to give me a second and I would be right back. They wanted to follow, but I said I could handle him on my own.

# Chapter Seven

## Malik

C yrus called me up to hang out at the club with him to keep an eye on Reece. At first, I didn't want to go, but then he mentioned my sister was there and Kash jumped at the chance to go out without being on baby duty since our parents offered to watch their son tonight. But seeing the sexy women out tonight, I might end up taking someone home since I hadn't dealt with Alyssa in a few weeks, or any other woman. Hearing the bass of a classic Biggie Smalls song creep through the speakers, I bounced my head and watched the women form a line on the floor twisting and swaying to the beat.

"Ladies and gentlemen, we have the legendary Cyrus Davidson and Kash Coleman in the house!" The DJ shouted over the microphone.

Cyrus tapped me on the shoulder and pointed toward the women upstairs in the VIP section.

"I see them," Cyrus said and stalked off toward them. I followed behind him looking around the club and noticed Sarai in the corner with some tall guy in front of her, and she looked pissed.

"I'll meet you guys up there," I told Kash.

"Where are you going?" he asked.

"I see Sarai and she doesn't look happy."

"You need us to come with you?" Kash asked.

"I can handle it," I answered, and he left to go sit with Reece and Arianna.

I nudged through as women tried to pull on me to talk with them, debating in my head if I should really do this since Sarai and I weren't exactly friends. We'd briefly talked in passing outside of work, and I was trying to push in on a situation I really had no right to interrupt. As I got closer, I heard him yelling about getting a second chance. So, he must be an ex-boyfriend of hers.

"What do you want me to do, Sarai? You and I both know we should be together," the guy insisted.

I walked up on them. "Sarai, you good?" I glanced between her and the guy, who was glaring at me.

Recognition dawned on her face and she tried to walk around him, and he held a hand up, blocking her from leaving.

"She's good, my guy," he said.

"I'm not your guy," I replied.

"Christopher, leave it alone and move on," Sarai told him.

"We need to talk, Sarai, alone," Christopher demanded, gripping her arm. I stepped in and pushed her behind me.

"The lady said to leave her alone," I told him.

"Who the fuck are you?" he asked.

"Christopher, don't make a scene. We both know it wouldn't be good for your image," Sarai said behind me.

"Fuck my career. Are you sleeping with him?" Christopher asked.

"No, and if I was, that's my business," Sarai argued back.

"Get over here, Sarai," Christopher announced.

"She's not going anywhere with you," I said.

He tried to reach around me and grab her and I gripped his shirt collar and pushed him against the wall.

"You must not understand when I say she's not going to be yours, motherfucker," I gritted through clenched teeth.

"Malik, let him go. He's not worth it and too many people are around," Sarai said as she touched my arm.

"Yo, Malik, you good?" I heard Cyrus shout. I peered over and saw him with security behind him.

"Are we good?" I asked Christopher and he nodded his head.

I let him go and he fixed his shirt and stepped back so he could walk away. He tried to call Sarai's name again and I held a hand to shut him up.

"Sarai, you starting trouble already?" Cyrus teased.

"Cyrus, don't start," she said.

"The publicist may need a publicist," Kash joked, and Sarai pushed him in the shoulder and stomped off toward the girls.

"You in the business of saving women you're not sleeping with now?" Cyrus inquired.

"She's a friend of Arianna's. I was being nice."

"Tell that lie to someone else," Cyrus taunted and wrapped his arm around my shoulder. The three of us hung out with the girls for the rest of the night and I kept my eyes on Sarai to see how she acted in a public setting when she wasn't working. The dress she was wearing left little to the imagination and if she was my woman, I'd probably hide that shit so she couldn't wear it again unless I was around.

"Stop staring," Arianna came over and said.

"What are you talking about, Ari?" I questioned.

"You're staring at Sarai. I can bet you're figuring out how many ways to get her to go home with you," Arianna commented.

"I don't like Sarai."

"I said the same thing about Kash and now look at me." Arianna rubbed her flat stomach.

"I doubt Sarai does one-night stands," I answered.

"Who told you that?" Arianna asked.

I scanned my eyes around the club and heard the DJ doing last call for drinks.

"Make sure you get him home and kiss my nephew for me."

"Are you coming to family dinner tomorrow?" Arianna asked as I stood up and kissed her forehead.

"I'll be there," I said and walked off to go down the stairs and out of the club. I was tempted to call up another woman, but something in my gut told me to leave it alone. I looked over my shoulder one more time and Sarai was staring at me as she sipped on her drink. I nodded and she mouthed thanks in answer. Taking my keys out of my pocket I headed toward my black viper two-seater and drove home to finish the night off with a bottle of scotch.

\* \* \*

The next morning, I woke up early to get a run in before I headed to the office to deal with Kendra and Asia. The park across the street from my condo was normally quiet around this time. I strapped up my shoes, plugged in my Air Pods, and started my way around the track to prepare for my day. Cicely would be arriving around seven to make breakfast and I'd be able to make it to the office by eight-thirty. I looked up and noticed Sarai stretching her legs and wearing biker shorts and a sports bra, bent over touching her toes.

"Why do I keep running into her?" I mumbled to myself. Since it was still pretty early and I'm not fond of it still being semi-dark, I approached her to see if she wanted to jog with me.

"We keep meeting like this," I muttered, surprising her, and she jumped back and held her hand to her chest, catching her breath.

"Sorry for scaring you," I said.

"What are you doing here, Malik? Are you following me?" Sarai queried as she looked around the area. I chuckled and shook my head no.

"Out for my morning run."

"I came out to run and never saw you out here," Sarai replied.

"Usually, you'll catch me on the other side."

"Ohh," Sarai said.

"You want to run together?" I asked.

"Uhm...sure."

She followed alongside me as I started jogging at a slow pace, keeping my focus in front of me and debating if I wanted to bring up last night.

"What time did you get in last night?" I questioned.

"Pretty much after you left," Sarai said.

"Who's your boyfriend?"

Sarai chortled. "That didn't last five minutes before you got in my business."

"I like to ask questions."

"Are you dating Asia?" She questioned, and I was taken aback at her constantly asking me about Asia. "She told my mom you guys were dating and that I'm trying to steal you."

I stopped jogging, placed my arms across my chest, and Sarai shrugged her shoulders like it wasn't a big deal her cousin was going around and lying about me.

"I'm not interested in Asia."

"I know, but she's in her own world and trying to find a rich guy to feed into her delusions," she said.

"I think it's time for me and Asia to have another conversation."

"I can talk with her for you."

"You're family and I hate to cause any issues between you two."

"She's young. I tried many times to help her out with finding work that fits her personality," Sarai told me.

"All Hands Homes is a great place to work at and to gain world experience," I said. We started running around the track again and a few more people showed up as the sun was rising.

"Yeah, I switch between Cyrus Premier Enterprises and Pierce Motors. Most of the time I work out of my main office in the city," Sarai stated.

"How did you end up working for Pierce Motors?"

"I forget we never had to deal with each other until the last year or so," Sarai remarked. That was true because most of the time I stayed more focused on the team and the business side and less on the celebrity side of things with the drivers.

"Once I started working with Cyrus, and from Reece's recommendations, I was introduced to Arianna and we hit it off. She asked me to meet with Jackson," Sarai explained.

"So, who do you think is better, Cyrus Premier Enterprises or Pierce Motors?" I joked.

"Never gonna answer that question," Sarai replied. I laughed and came upon a bench and stopped to sit down to catch my breath and talk more.

"That dude Christopher your ex?" I queried again. She nodded and sat down next to me.

"He is and he thinks we should get back together. It doesn't help that my mom loves him," Sarai explained.

I checked my watch. "Listen, let's finish this conversation at my place," I said and noticed her brow raise in suspicion.

"Cicely is arriving right about now to make me breakfast and you know she makes more than enough food."

"No thanks."

"Why are you scared?" My tongue darted out to lick my dry lips.

"I don't know, Malik. I hate to impose, and besides, we've never been the best of friends," Sarai commented. I held my hand out and she looked down at it in surprise.

"Hi, I'm Malik Pierce. VP of Pierce Motors, uncle to two spoiled kids, and middle child of Chavonne and Eddison Sr."

She smirked and extended a hand out to me.

"Sarai Lambert, CEO and Owner of Lambert Publicity Services. Daughter of DeeDee Lambert," Sarai explained as we walked back to our building.

"If you don't mind me asking, where's your father?"

"Either running around living his life or dead."

"Grew up with a single mom?" I questioned as I peered over at her as we crossed the street. Once at the building, I held the door open so she could walk inside. The receptionist and security waved at us and I nodded back as we stepped on the elevator for our ride to the penthouse section.

"And I'm an only child. At least you had your brother and sister growing up," Sarai mentioned.

Finally, we stepped off the elevator and she followed me toward my door. I pulled the keys out of my pocket and opened the door, smelling coffee, bacon, and cinnamon rolls for breakfast. The tv was playing the early morning news and Cicely waved at me as she placed a plate down on my table.

"I wasn't expecting two people for breakfast," Cicely said, grinning from ear to ear. I smirked, pointing at Cicely, and walked into the kitchen and kissed her cheek.

"Ohh you stink. Go shower and come back to eat," Cicely blurted out and shoved me away. I smelled under my arm and sniffed the musk from working out and laughed at her harsh scoff.

"See how she treats me?" I asked Sarai and pointed at Cicely.

Sarai chuckled and went to sit down at the table to eat.

"You do stink." In response, Sarai picked up a plate and fork before diving into a breakfast of cinnamon rolls and bacon.

"You come into my house and insult me, Sarai?"

Cicely stepped closer and pushed me away to go change.

"Your food will get cold. Hurry up and change," Cicely stated.

I grabbed a piece of bacon and ran to the back to shower and change. I kicked off my shoes, removed my shirt, and dumped it in the hamper next to my bathroom.

I picked up the large towel Cicely left for me on my bed and removed my pants to head into the bathroom when I realized I left my shower gel in the guest bathroom from when my niece and nephew stayed over and I let them use my products. I walked out of my bedroom and bumped into Sarai with my bare chest and a towel wrapped around my waist. I wrapped my hands around her waist, pulling her in close to keep her from falling to the ground.

# Chapter Eight

## Malik

"Sorry, I was trying to get to the bathroom," Sarai said as her eyes scanned down my face to my chest. She took in a harsh breath.

"Of course. It's down the hall to the left."

"I think you have to let me go, Malik," Sarai stated.

I realized I was still holding onto her waist and gently pushed her away from me before she could feel my girth rising on her thigh.

"Yeah. That would help. Can you pass the shower gel to me?" I asked as I followed behind her.

I slowly licked my lips, staring at her ass as she walked into my guest bathroom.

"You stare any longer you'll look like a stalker," Cicely joked.

"What are you talking about, old lady?" I tried to back up when she smacked me on the back of the head.

"Act stupid if you want to," Cicely said and walked away as Sarai came back out with the bodywash and passed it to me. Sarai held it in her hands and I wrapped my hand underneath hers, and we both stood there lingering as we gazed into each other's eyes.

"I need to get in the shower before work. You're more than welcome to join me in the shower," I said.

"I'm starting to stink myself. I think I should head out to my place now before I end up here all day and see you later on," Sarai announced before doing what she said then heading out of my place to go next door. I went back to the bathroom, turned on the shower, checked the temperature, and stepped inside, closing the door. I stood underneath the water and let the scorching heat fall down my back and I thought of what my day would be like once I had another conversation with Asia. There was a light tap on my door and I heard Cicely calling from the other side.

"Yeah!" My voice rang out.

"Alyssa wants to talk to you."

"Tell her I'm busy."

"She said call her or she'll show up here."

I groaned and finished washing my body and clearing the soap off my legs and stepped out of the shower and picked up the towel off the counter to dry off. Brushing my teeth again, I finished by rubbing lotion on, putting on deodorant, then throwing on a shirt and boxers. Marching out of the bathroom to pick out a suit for the day, I finally decided on plain black slacks with a black shirt and no tie. Twenty minutes later, I walked out of my bedroom to grab something to eat and drink a cup of coffee before leaving out.

"She sounded pissed," Cicely said.

"Alyssa is just mad I ended things with her." I picked up the newspaper and went to the sports section and saw a front-page mention of the charity race that

Pierce Motors and Cyrus Premier Enterprises were hosting.

"Will you be at a family dinner tonight?" Cicely questioned.

"Yes, ma'am," I answered, took a sip of my coffee, picked up the rolls, and stood up to leave for the day.

"I'll see you tonight and try to not fall too deep in love with Sarai," Cicely joked, and I kissed her on the cheek, walked over to pick up my keys off the table in the living room, and left.

\* \* \*

An hour later I pulled into my parking space at Pierce Motors and turned the car off and chucked my chin up at a few of the guards on duty. I stopped at the front entrance and talked with the receptionist and security about how things were going for the morning. I got a rundown of any issues and they told me Asia was out front talking with paparazzi a few minutes ago.

"Thanks, guys," I said, sighing before I stomped to the elevator to head to my office. I pulled out my phone to check for messages and saw Cyrus messaged me about doing another poker night. As the elevator dinged, I walked out and replied.

*Me: I can't tonight. Family dinner.*

*Cyrus: Cool, call me to reschedule.*

*Me: Sounds good.*

I closed out of my phone and walked up to Kendra's desk.

"Where's Asia?" I demanded.

"She went to the bathroom. Why?" Kendra asked.

"Send her to my office as soon as she gets back."

"What happened? Did she mess something up?" Kendra wondered and followed behind me. I opened the door to my office and dropped my keys on top of the desk, then sat in my chair and leaned back, lifting my hand to my cheek in thought.

"You look pissed and I don't like it," Kendra said.

"Asia was out front talking to paparazzi and running around saying we're dating."

"She said this to the paparazzi?" Kendra questioned.

"I don't know, but she told Sarai."

"Her cousin Sarai?" Kendra asked and I nodded in answer.

I heard a knock at my door and I looked around at Asia holding two cups of coffee.

"Hey, Malik, I got your favorite drink with two sugars," Asia said, walking in and handing me the cup. Kendra stayed standing and looked from me to Asia. I placed the cup down and motioned for Asia to take a seat.

"What were you doing talking to the paparazzi?" I asked.

"Nothing," Asia replied, taking a sip of her latte, and crossing her leg.

"Asia, you've barely been here two months and have already caused me annoyance."

# Chapter Nine

## Malik

She looked at Kendra and back at me, her face flushed in embarrassment. I gave people plenty of chances, but she was going overboard with fucking with my business.

"I don't know what you've heard, Malik," Asia said.

"Security told me you were spotted talking to the paparazzi and it looked like something was exchanged."

"Like money?" Kendra questioned.

"Good question," I wondered.

Asia shifted in her seat as she glanced from me to Kendra. Terror overtook her face.

"Uhm...it's...not like that," Asia said.

"What's it like, Asia?"

"I was trying to secure an interview for you with *Business Magazine*," Asia lied right to my face, and I let her continue. I leaned forward and clasped my hands together, taking in everything she was mentioning.

"So, let me get this straight. You thought talking with a member of the paparazzi would somehow get me an opportunity with a magazine?"

"I know it sounds crazy, but I figured if they saw you in your environment, they would approach me about an interview once the photos got out and I would possibly get named," Asia mentioned.

I chortled because I knew something was behind her little confession.

"You getting recognition is what this is all about, not me."

"Asia, the only way you move up here at Pierce Motors is by working as a team player," Kendra said. Asia nodded her head and jumped up to leave.

"Do you need anything right now, Malik?" Asia asked.

"No, you've done enough."

Asia sighed and walked out of my office. I could have sworn she rolled her eyes, but I'd save that for another day. Kendra took a seat right as Jackson came to my door.

"Glad to see you both here," Jackson commented, coming inside.

Jackson extended his hand for a shake and I reciprocated.

"What's going on, cousin?"

"I finished meeting with Canon and he showed me the proofs from Arianna's shoot," Jackson said as he slipped his hands in his pockets.

"They look great."

"I'm impressed and think you do a great job. I signed off on the paperwork for you to be CEO once I retire," Jackson announced. Kendra gasped in excitement.

"You seriously want to retire?" I questioned.

"I do, but I'll still keep an eye on you though," Jackson joked. "You're built for this. I know you wanted to play sports professionally, but you're built for this business side," Jackson stated.

"Thanks, what are you about to get into?"

"I need to leave for a meeting with JJ's teacher," he replied, reminding me of why he wanted to be home more since he and Emery had four kids now.

"Tell Emery I said hello and make sure you're at the game tomorrow night."

"I'll be there with bells on and taking your money," Jackson joked.

"Jackson, give the kids a kiss for me," Kendra remarked as she smiled up at him.

Jackson's mouth quirked up at the mention of his kids, as he walked out of my office. The man used to be a bachelor until one day he came to family dinner and said he'd met this woman and fell in love after one day.

"What?" I asked as Kendra glared at me.

"Fire her," Kendra stated.

"I thought you loved her," I remarked, and she waved me off.

"I was wrong, she's been doing little sneaky stuff around here and I tried to play it off that she was just trying to fit in, but now this paparazzi situation has me rethinking my earlier thoughts," Kendra told me.

"What has she done? You keep me out of the loop on everything." I ran a hand down my face in frustration.

"Whenever someone tried to do something for you or prepare for a meeting that you had, Asia would get pissed and snap at them," Kendra said, and I'm surprised she never told me all of the stuff Asia was doing.

"Anything else?"

"She's taking longer breaks, talking on the office

phone when she should be working," Kendra muttered lowly.

"Wait...you're telling me that Asia has basically been hanging out when I'm not around?"

"To an extent, yes," Kendra said.

"Why didn't you tell me earlier?"

"Malik, you've been a little distracted with work and women," Kendra said.

"Kendra, you know me better than anyone. If my business is compromised, we need to fix the issue. I refuse to put my cousin's company in a bad light."

"I agree," Kendra replied.

"We're too close to launching the clothing line and charity race. Move Asia closer to your desk and give her paperwork to deal with," I demanded as she stood up to leave.

"Anything else?"

"I don't give too many chances often; I know she's young, so I'll let her get this one last chance," I answered, and Kendra walked out of my office leaving the door open. I heard her tell Asia to handle filing a stack of paperwork that just got dropped off with sponsorship potentials for Pierce Motors. Once I was alone, I continued handling phone calls and business throughout the day as everyone wanted my time when they found out I was working. I had lunch at my desk and continued going over projections for next year while eating my burger and fries. My cell phone vibrated on the desk.

Alyssa: Please talk to me.

Me: What do you want?

Alyssa: I made a mistake.

Me: We both did.

Alyssa: Don't say it like that.

*Me: I'm working Alyssa.*

*Alyssa: Can I see you tonight?*

*Me: I can't. I have my family dinner.*

Which reminded me I needed to make sure my brother had them ready when I picked them up tonight. I planned on stopping by my parents to scoop them up to spend the night with me since it was going on the weekend and the women were leaving on vacation.

*Alyssa: That's fine, we can just talk.*

*Me: You know I don't allow anyone at my folks place.*

*Alyssa: Malik, please baby. I miss you.*

*Me: I'll think about it.*

I closed out of my phone and continued on for the rest of the day as Canon dropped by with the top pictures he thought would play well for the marketing launch of our clothing line.

* * *

Later in the day, I was driving over to my parents house and listening to sports radio discussing our upcoming race and the industry in general.

"Cyrus Premier Enterprises is legendary and Pierce Motors is closely coming up with the drivers they have," Peter, the talk show host, stated.

"I agree. Cyrus placed Kash in a great position as the center of the industry and now Arianna is leading as the top female driver," Ryan, the co-host, said.

Turning down the street of my parents home, I saw my brother, Eddison Jr.'s or EJ for short car in the driveway. I parked on the street and slid the key out of the ignition and stepped out still wearing my suit jacket. I checked my watch and saw it was going on six-thirty, so they should be sitting down for dinner. I used my key to open the door and saw Cicely and my mom talking in the archway of the dining room.

"What are you two gossiping about?" I asked. Cicely and my mom, Chavonne, grinned when they saw me.

"Hey, sweetie, you know your momma doesn't gossip," my mother stated. I smirked knowing she was lying through her teeth.

"Speak for yourself, Chavonne," Cicely remarked and hugged me and I laughed out loud at the scowl on my mother's face.

"Close your mouth before a fly gets inside," I teased.

"Uncle Malik!" My niece and nephew ran over and yelled. I picked up Madison and kissed her cheek and rubbed the top of Major's head.

"Hey, princess," I said to her.

"Are you ready to go?" She asked with both her hands on my face to make sure I was focused on her. I chuckled at her being a little diva like my sister and wondered what guy thought he was going to come in and sweep her off her feet when she got older.

"Princess, can I say hi to my parents before we go?" I asked, smiling at her cute little face. She pulled her tiny hand to her cheek like she was thinking about my request.

"All right," Madison told me and squirmed out of my hold. I bent down to dap up Major.

"What's going on, little man?" I questioned him and he grinned, showing off the two dimples in his cheeks.

"Uncle Malik, you got a dollar?" He asked, holding out a hand.

"I do."

"Can I have ten then?" Major asked.

Cicely, Mom, and I all burst into laughter.

"Why did you ask me for a dollar at first?"

"So when you give me the ten, you'll still have money in your pocket," Major said like it made sense and we should all be thinking like him. I shook my head and pulled out my wallet and found two five-dollar bills and passed them to him.

"Me too!" Madison jumped up and down screaming.

"See what you started?" Eddison Jr. said. My older brother looked just like our father.

"I didn't expect to get swindled so early," I said then followed behind them into the dining room. My dad was sitting at the table eating his dinner. He must have come home early from the office. He had been talking about retiring soon from Pierce Motors to travel with my mom.

"What did you cook, Ma?" I asked.

"Cicely made cabbage and pork chops and I did the salad, wraps, and pasta," Mom explained.

"I had a big lunch already and I know Cicely left me something at home."

"You know it," Cicely stated. I looked around at the chocolate cake and lemon cake on the table.

"Thanks, fam, but let me get out of here so I hang with my crew. Madison and Major, grab your jackets."

They ran off to gather their bags and I talked with my brother and father about my day at work and what was going on with the clothing line. Arianna called as we left to say she was getting ready to put little Kash to bed and pack for her trip tomorrow. I walked out of the house, following behind the kids, and helped them in the car, locking their seatbelts. Thirty minutes later I was sitting at home, wearing black sweats and a t-shirt. I finally got them to agree to watching the latest Marvel movie. The popcorn and lemonade were next to us. Madison painted my fingernails while my nephew acted out the scene in front of Chris Evans character.

"Get him, Captain America," Major screamed.

"He's so childish," Madison mumbled, and I cackled at her comment as she fanned my hand.

"You like this color?" Madison asked.

"Yeah, baby, it's cool," I said.

"Cool...You mean cute, Uncle Malik," Madison said.

"What's wrong with cool?"

"Girls say cute and boys say cool," Madison remarked.

"She's right, Uncle Malik," Major told me.

"Well I'm going to say cool and you two have thirty more minutes before you head to bed," I said. The both of them groaned as the front door buzzed. I looked over at the clock on the stand and it read nine o'clock. I stood up and walked toward the front door, checking the peephole and seeing Alyssa on the other side. I grunted and looked back at the kids to make sure they were distracted with the TV. I tried to calm my nerves before going off on this girl for dropping by my place without calling first. I never gave her my address so she must have done some under-handed shit to find me. I opened the door with a harsh glare on my face and saw that Alyssa was wearing a trench coat and I assumed lingerie underneath.

I stepped out and slightly closed the door behind me.

"What are you doing here?"

"Hey, baby," Alyssa said as she tried to reach her arms around my head.

"Alyssa, how did you find my place?"

"I have friends in high places," Alyssa said.

"Before I have you arrested, tell me exactly why you're here."

"I think it's time we made things serious between us."

"Alyssa, our agreement was sex and nothing else. You can't switch it up now that you've caught feelings."

"Are you saying you don't feel anything for me?" Alyssa asked and opened her coat, showing off her two-piece lingerie set with thigh-high stockings and a thong that was barely hiding her mound. I heard laughing coming from the living room, reminding me of my guests.

"You need to go and don't come back here again. I'm done."

"Who's in there with you?" Alyssa tried to walk inside, and I blocked her with my hand on the door.

"Grow up and go home. I'm not interested anymore and if you come here again, I'll have you arrested," I announced and watched the corners of her lower lip tremble. Alyssa wiped the tear before it dropped down her cheek, closed her coat, and stomped toward the elevator to leave. I turned and walked back inside my condo and scooped up my niece to place her in my lap.

"Fifteen more minutes, rugrats."

"Okay!" they both shouted and cuddled up next to me. I ended up watching the rest of the movie on my own because they fell asleep ten minutes later. I carried them both to the guest room and put them under the covers and turned the light off. Picking up the bowl of popcorn and lemonade, I took it to the kitchen and tossed the rest in the garbage. Deciding to clean up in the morning, I headed to bed to get some sleep before work.

# Chapter Ten

## Sarai

**T**wo days later.

I was working late in the office at Pierce Motors going over details for the big charity race. My eyes were getting heavy, but I needed to push through and lay out the correct line up for the press and seating chart of who was invited.

The cleaning crew was tossing away trash and I stood up, grabbing my cup to go make another pot of coffee. I wasn't planning on leaving anytime soon since I technically told Malik it would be ready by the time I got back from our trip.

"Sarai, you're still here?" Janet asked, wiping down the receptionist's desk.

"Yeah, I wanted to get something taken care of before I left."

"Well at least you're not the only one here late," Janet told me.

"Who else is here?" I flattened down a tuft of hair.

"Boss man is here, Mr. Pierce."

"Oh... well, let me stop talking so you finish working.

I heard he can be a hard ass," I whispered teasingly, and she laughed. I headed in the kitchen and saw a fresh brew and I smiled, gripped the side, and poured the remnants in my cup. I stood on my toes to grab the cinnamon from the cabinet when I heard someone clearing their throat.

"Hey," I said and tried to look for the stool to grab the cinnamon. They always put things on the highest shelf.

"What happened to my drink?" Malik asked.

"I don't know." He angled a glance down at me. I slid mine behind me.

"Are you trying to hide something, Sarai?" Malik asked, reaching around me to grab the cup.

"Hey that's mine!" I put my hands on my hips.

"No, it's mine because I made it and you came in here and stole it."

"I didn't steal anything, you should have made enough for everybody," I snapped and tried to grab it back.

"It's only me working," he rasped.

"Uhm...I wonder how you got the position of not being good at math. I'm working tonight as well," I bellowed as he took a sip of my drink.

"Then you should have made another cup. That's the polite office thing to do." Malik's voice was laced with irritation.

"Oh my god! Why are you like this? Do your parents even like you?" I questioned, grabbed another filter, and started making another pot.

"Here, you can have it back and I'll make another pot," Malik told me and I flipped him off.

"No thanks. I don't know where your lips have been."

"Somewhere where you've probably only dreamed

about," Malik stated as he opened the fridge and picked up the carton of milk.

"You probably wouldn't even know how to eat pussy. The preppy type never does," I mumbled and chortled. My heart rate kicked up a notch when I felt his breath tickling my ear. I closed my eyes for a second, trying to concentrate on scooping enough grounds for two cups of coffee.

"You can't mumble for shit. I suggest you not comment on something you know nothing about."

"I've heard enough. You're the player type," I muttered.

"I can bet fifty dollars right now your pussy is begging for me to put my tongue on it and ease the ache. Tell me, Sarai, when was the last time a man had your legs bent back to your ears?" Malik questioned.

"Damn," Janet blurted out and covered her mouth as we caught her at the doorway. Malik stepped back, and I cleared my throat, taking the coffee out of his hands and leaving the kitchen.

"Have a good night, Janet," I heard Malik say behind me.

I went back to my office and for the next hour finished working on my list of gift bags we'd need to order until it was time to head home and go to sleep. I hopped in my car and made it home in less than twenty minutes and jumped out, running inside. The doorman tried to speak but I waved him off. I was still hot and sexually aroused by Malik and needed a cold shower to relieve the stimulation. I tossed everything down as soon as I got in and went toward my bedroom and opened my drawer to use my little friend.

Half an hour later, I was sleeping peacefully in bed.

# Chapter Eleven

## Sarai

The next afternoon I was boarding Cyrus's private jet for our girls trip and Essence decided to join us. I guess she was going through something with one of her guy friends. I passed by Arianna and sat down across from her, wearing a one-piece black bathing suit with a high waistline and plunging neckline with a see-through wrap that tied at my waist. I planned on thoroughly enjoying myself before work really exploded for me once I got back. The stewardess walked over with a tray of champagne in her hand. I picked up a glass and tasted the pineapple and strawberry flavors.

"This is good," I commented.

"It's nonalcoholic," Arianna stated.

"I forgot you couldn't drink," I stated, watching Reece come over and sit down next to me. She'd texted everyone in the group chat to wear our bathing suits because once we got off the plane we'd head out shopping and then to brunch. Gabriella and Essence were in the next section of seats and Gabriella had her phone on speaker talking with her kids.

"Momma, make sure you bring me something back," Madison told her, and she chuckled.

"Did you have fun with Uncle Malik?" Gabriella questioned.

"Yes and he burnt my pancakes," Madison whispered over the phone, and we all laughed.

"Princess, why did you tell your mom that? I thought that was our little secret," Malik's boisterous voice came through the phone.

"Madison can't keep a secret, Malik. I should have told you that," Gabriella remarked.

"I see," Malik replied.

"Uncle Malik, this is a girl talking," Madison commented.

"Sorry, princess," Malik answered, his voice raspy. Something about his voice was calming yet demanding at the same time.

"When is Eddison coming to get them? I know they're driving you crazy," Gabriella stated.

"He should be here soon. They're not bothering me. It helps to have Kendra and Asia here to help when I need to step out for a meeting," Malik advised, and I chortled unintentionally and all eyes looked at me.

"Who is that?" Malik questioned, and I covered my mouth in embarrassment.

"Oh...Sarai," Gabriella stated.

Malik chuckled over the phone and I wanted to smack the knowing smirk I knew was on his face.

"Hi, Malik!" Reece yelled out.

"Hey, ladies, make sure you don't get out of control out there," Malik said.

"We promise," all of them answered at the same time.

"Sarai." Malik called out my name.

All of the girls looked at me perplexed and I shrugged my shoulders, shocked right along with them about Malik calling my name.

"Yes?" I answered.

"Try not to get into any trouble," Malik remarked.

"I can't promise that," I replied.

"Are you making a promise to me now?" He questioned.

"Of course not. I was just saying we can't promise we will behave."

"I only asked *you* to behave," Malik said.

"Do you two need to be alone?" Gabriella inquired.

"Gabriella, don't play me," I said and took another sip of my drink.

Malik chuckled and said goodbye to everybody right as the door was closing and the seatbelt sign came on.

"Cyrus told me they have guys night at Malik's," Reece informed them as she turned off her phone.

"Kash said he was going tonight," Arianna said.

"What do they do at these guys nights?" I questioned.

"Nothing much besides play poker, drink, and talk about women," Reece stated.

"Y'all cool with that?"

"No different than us talking about men when we get together," Reece commented, and I nodded in agreement because that was true. We always discussed what was going on in our lives. Most of the time I left my sex life out of things.

"What happened with you the other night at the club? Cyrus told me Christopher had you in the corner and was screaming at you," Reece asked, reminding me of something I tried to forget. I had blocked him from my phone, but he always found a way to get in touch.

"He was talking about how he wants to try again like I'm some young girl that will accept the disrespect." I chortled, drinking the rest of my fruity drink.

"Cyrus told me that security watched as he walked out of the club upset from Malik embarrassing him," Arianna said.

"Christopher has the biggest ego on the planet," I said. The plane left the runway and we continued talking, eating small snacks while laughing at pictures of little Kash playing at the track.

\* \* \*

Five hours later we arrived at the beach house in the Bahamas, stepped out of the car, and carried our bags inside.

"Ladies, you all have your own private room with your name on the door," Reece stated.

"Nice, because I planned on bringing a man back to my room," Essence announced, and we laughed at her rubbing her hands together in excitement.

"No men, Essence. If you need to get your rocks off, hotel only," Reece told her.

"That's messed up, Reece," Essence commented.

"No that's Cyrus's rules. He only agreed if I made sure no guys would be here," Reece confessed.

"That's easy for you to say, most of y'all got husbands and boyfriends. Me and Sarai are single and ready to mingle," Essence spoke up, bringing me into her drama.

I waved my hand. "Keep me out of your single ladies speech please."

"Sarai, for once, pick a side," Essence demanded and plopped facedown on the couch groaning.

"This girls trip was meant for us to relax," I said.

"Can we go shopping because I'm starving?" Arianna asked, rubbing her flat stomach.

"Yes. Essence, the men will probably be at the mall, so calm your hot butt down," Reece joked and took her bag into her room. I followed behind and dropped my bag in the room across from hers. I slid my hand in my purse and checked to make sure I had my shades and wallet before I strolled to the front to leave.

"What do you plan on buying, Sarai?" Reece questioned as she placed her shades on and returned a text.

"Is that Cyrus checking up on you?" I teased.

"Yes, I guess Malik told him that we talked to him," Reece replied.

"I want dresses and maybe some short sets," I answered as I followed her to the Lincoln Town Car SUV. The driver held the door open and I jumped inside behind her as Arianna, Essence, and Gabriella came out of the house.

"That'd be cute, I want to get a mixture of everything," Reece told me.

"Have you got your dress for the charity race yet?" I asked.

"I have a red dress that I'm eyeing, but I might wear something else," Reece explained.

"Reece, are the boys coming to the charity dinner again?" Arianna inquired.

"I need to check and see. I wasn't planning on bringing them though."

"Cyrus probably wants you all to himself that night," Essence teased, wiggling her tongue out as she burst into laughter.

"Worry about your own man. Tripp coming with you?" Reece asked.

"Nope," Essence said.

"What! Ohh tell us the gossip, boo," Arianna investigated.

"I'm just exploring my options, that's all," Essence retorted.

The car pulled off and we drove out to the local marketplace to shop. Grabbing authentic pieces would be awesome and maybe I could pick up some new clients if the clothes look good.

"Sarai, you never told us what's going on with your love life," Gabriella said.

"I have no love life, Gabriella."

"So, you and Malik weren't flirting a little while ago?"

I cleared my throat and sat up straight in my seat.

"I don't call that flirting. How long have you been married again?" I joked.

"Could have fooled us," Essence blurted out as the car turned into the marketplace and parked.

"Malik is my client and that's it," I stated and opened my door, forgetting to take off my seatbelt.

"He got you forgetting how to get out of the seat." Arianna pointed at me. I flipped her off and unbuckled the seatbelt, stepping out and hearing the beats and drums of music. Essence and Reece followed and started clapping their hands to the beats.

"I need a few cocktails and some of that tall, dark, and handsome man over there," Essence announced, pointing at a guy pouring water over his head from the heat. He stood about six-four or five, was muscular in build, had a rich, dark brown skin tone, and was wearing athletic biker pants with no shirt.

"Now that's a workout I'm willing to endure," I joked as I licked my lips.

"No, ma'am, you already have a man. Hell, you have two," Essence remarked and tried to walk toward him. Reece pulled her back.

"I don't have a man and I'd appreciate you not spreading that rumor."

"Christopher and Malik are both sniffing at your door," Essence said, picking up the glasses from the woman standing in front of the sunglasses booth. The entire booth showcased different designs with low prices.

"Essence, focus on your own problems with Tripp. Reece, let's go to the dress shop over there," I spoke and entwined my arm in hers and we went to the store. I picked up a black short knee length and held it up to my chin and looked in the mirror.

"What do you think of this?" I asked Reece.

"A little short and you have way more up top to cover, honey," Reece stated, and I pouted, putting it back. She was right about my breasts being a nice, healthy size that would spill over in the top part. I continued picking through the clothes when she held up a colorful blue and white striped dress.

"I like this one," Reece said, and pushed it forward.

"That would be cute, especially with your hair up in a high bun," I said, holding her hair up as she looked in the wall mirror next to the checkout stand. The busy crowd of tourists and music playing made me want to stay more than a week.

"What about this one?" I lifted the long sleeve peach color for her to look at.

"That would be so cute on you. It'd have Malik running behind you trying to keep tabs," Reece taunted.

"Why is everybody constantly bringing him up to me?"

We circled around the store and I finally decided on the peach one and a pair of flat shoes to match. Taking it up to the register, I paid and thanked them as we left to catch up to Arianna and the rest of the girls.

"Reminds me of Cyrus and me when we started," Reece told me.

"I forgot about you two lovebirds."

"It wasn't always like that, in the beginning I thought he was this stuck up celebrity playboy," Reece reminisced.

"And what do you think now?"

"I think he's the best thing that ever happened to me and we challenge each other to be better," Reece told me.

"Thanks, great for you, but your girl is not looking for love."

"Sarai, you sound like me when I first started dating Kamden," Arianna said, wrapping her arm around my shoulder. Essence and Gabriella ate ice cream as we walked down the market.

"I still have nightmares about that Vegas one-night stand," I blurted out. Arianna shoved me away and I laughed.

"Leave my baby alone," Arianna stated, picking up a pair of shoes at the next shop on the street.

"We all have nightmares about how you two came together. Have you heard anything about Ralph and Josie?" Reece asked.

"Last time I heard they were still in jail," Arianna commented.

"Good," Essence stated.

"I want to do a bet," Gabriella stated.

I pointed at the restaurant next to the beach to stop in and eat while we watched the waves. The girls followed me.

"What kind of bet?" Reece asked.

"I bet a hundred bucks that Sarai sleeps with Malik and falls in love," Gabriella said, and I stopped in my tracks.

"Ohh...I'm in on that bet." Essence excitedly went in her purse to pull out some money.

"Gabriella, you of all people. I see where Madison gets it from."

"Leave my baby out of this and I'm just having a little fun," Gabriella said.

"I'm in for two hundred," Arianna said. My mouth dropped in shock that my best friend was betting on my love life.

"Hello, how many for dinner?" the hostess asked. Reece held up a hand for five and she grabbed some menus to escort us to our table.

"Can we get a table by the water?" Reece asked.

"Sure, would this be okay?" the hostess asked and put us up front facing the water. I sat at the end so I was sideways to the table and could see my surroundings.

"You can call off your bets because I'm not sleeping with him or anyone else," I spat, picking up the cloth napkin and placing it in my lap. Arianna giggled and picked up her phone to FaceTime Kamden.

"I think it could be fun. Malik is fine, Sarai," Essence said.

"I didn't say he wasn't, but he's not my type."

"What the sexy, tall, dependable, and humble type?" Gabriella retorted.

"You have to say that, Gabriella, you're the sister-in-law," I answered and rolled my eyes.

"Hey, baby," Arianna said into the phone.

"When are you coming home?" Kash asked. Arianna laughed at his pitiful plea.

"Kash, you can't go one week without your wife?" I taunted. Arianna moved the phone toward me and I noticed he wasn't alone. A group of guys in the background were yelling and laughing. Looked like a casino was happening in the living room.

"Sarai, stay out of this. I blame you for wanting to do a damn *Stella Got Her Groove Back* vacation and stealing my wife," Kash said. My mouth dropped in shock as everyone started laughing, including the men surrounding him. When he stood up to walk away from the table, he headed into a kitchen that looked somewhat like mine, which told me he was at Malik's.

"Kash, don't get your feelings hurt in front of your wife," I challenged as his eyebrows dipped in a hard glare.

Malik patted Kash on the shoulder. "Who are you talking to?" Kash moved the phone to show me and I bit my bottom lip taking in his appearance. He wore a fitted black t-shirt that showed off his muscles and black jeans. It was the second time I had seen him in casual clothes.

"Sarai kidnapped my wife," Kamden joked. Arianna tittered and covered her mouth while I waved him off.

"I told Arianna that the girls trip was a setup," Malik cautioned, picking up the beer bottle off the counter and taking a sip.

"A setup for who?" I demanded, possibly falling into the trap of an argument.

"When women get together, it's probably all about bashing the men," Malik commented.

"Malik, leave Sarai alone," Arianna stated.

"Is Cyrus there?" Reece blurted out.

Kash passed the phone over to Cyrus as they walked back toward the living room.

"Hey, Cyrus," I said.

"Sarai, is everything good?"

"Yes, but you already knew that with the gorgeous home you put us in for our stay," I explained.

"Where's Reece?"

Arianna passed the phone to Reece and she blew him a kiss.

"Hey," Reece said.

"You need something?" Cyrus asked.

"No, we're fine. We just finished shopping and now we're eating on the beach," Reece told him.

"Make sure you call me before you go to bed," Cyrus stated, and Reece smiled and handed the phone back to Arianna.

"Bye, Cyrus," Arianna said and hung up the phone.

The waitress came over to our table with glasses of water and straws. She placed one in front of us all and I took a sip and prepared to try something from the menu.

# Chapter Twelve

## Sarai

Heida, our waitress, jotted down Arianna and Reece's order then she came behind me and asked what I would like to order. I flipped the menu around and ordered yellow bird, conch salad, and rock lobsters.

"Anything else you need?" Heida asked, picking up our menus. We let her know we were good and settled in to wait for our food. I grabbed a piece of bread and slathered it in warm butter and popped it in my mouth.

"I'm starving. I hope this food is good," Gabriella said.

"If the food is bad, please don't go into chef mode and try to tell them how to cook," Essence remarked.

"A chef can never turn it off," Gabriella responded, cutting into the bread.

"I should have gotten a sweater, it's chilly now," Reece commented, and I nodded in agreement. The sun was going down and we sat close to the beach to watch the waves and kids run around in the sand.

"All right, we have the conch salad and yellow bird," Heida said and I pointed at myself.

Another waitress came around and placed the rest of the plates down in front of the other girls.

"Thank you," Arianna stated.

"Cheers, ladies, this is for our girls trip," Reece spoke up, holding up her drink, and we clanked glasses.

"Let me try a little of your salad, Sarai," Arianna requested. I passed my plate over so she could take a few bites.

"Mmmmm...this is good," Arianna said, pointing at my salad, and I agreed as I held up a high five.

"I won't be able to finish all of this, so I'll need a to-go plate," I said.

Essence joked about meeting more guys on the rest of the trip and Gabriella ended up ordering another plate of shellfish as we continued talking and drinking. After two hours we ended up back at the house, knocked out in our rooms from the long travel day.

* * *

Three days later, we decided to go scuba diving and ride jet skis. I wore a two-piece pink bathing suit and was currently listening to the instructor tell us the proper way to scuba dive as well as the safety protocols. Tightening my vest under my wetsuit I was preparing to knock off one more thing on my bucket list. Reece and I were going first and then Essence and Gabriella. Arianna decided to stay back at the house since she was still tired from the pregnancy and partying the night before.

"Ready to go?" Instructor Thomas asked.

"Yes!" Reece and I said at the same time.

Taylor counted off and we dove underwater with our new friends. He showed us the different facets of water life. Seeing the different shells and rocks, and the colorful exploration of how things are inhabited once it deteriorates underwater, was an experience.

An hour later, we drove back to the house talking about our time and looking at the photos we took at the beach. As the car pulled in the driveway, we saw Arianna standing on the front porch talking on the phone and it looked intense. The driver parked the car and we jumped out, and I stopped in front of her to see what was happening.

"She's here now," Arianna said.

"You all right?" I questioned.

"Okay...Malik, let me call you back," Arianna told him and hung up.

"Something wrong with lil Kash?" Reece asked.

"That was Malik. Shit has hit the fan and it has to do with your cousin," Arianna said.

I groaned and put my hand on my hips ready to hear what Asia had done.

"She's accusing Malik of using her for sex and then firing her afterwards," Arianna stated, and my eyes rose in shock.

"I'm sorry, what?"

"Malik wouldn't do something like that," Reece said, and I agreed with her. Knowing how Asia moved and the amount of drama that followed her, I could bet he probably turned her down and she was doing this for money.

"Asia did an interview with Diamond blog and it's all over social media," Arianna informed.

"Let me see your phone," I said. Arianna passed it over and I checked every social media site. It was the top trending topic—Malik Pierce of Pierce Motors fired Asia Lambert after a one-night stand.

"Wow," Reece said over my shoulder.

I dialed Asia to see what was going on.

"Yeah," Asia answered dryly.

"Asia, what are you doing?" I asked.

"I don't know what you're talking about."

"This accusation about Malik. Do you understand you're running his name through the mud?" I questioned.

"You didn't even ask if it's true or not!" Asia yelled.

"Is it?"

"Yes, we slept together," Asia spat.

"Okay, so why are you pushing this on social media?"

"Because he can't go around just sleeping with women and then dropping us like my feelings don't mean anything."

"Asia, at any point did he say you guys were a couple?"

I heard the phone beep, so I told her to hold on and then answered the call on the other end.

"Arianna, let me talk to Sarai," Malik's deep voice called out.

"This is Sarai."

"Your cousin has lost her mind," Malik grumbled.

"What happened, Malik?"

"Nothing. She asked me out once again and I said no. Then she tried to kiss me and I pushed her off me," Malik said, and my eyebrows furrowed in confusion.

I held a hand up for Arianna to let me use her phone a little longer and she nodded okay.

"So, you two never slept together?" I asked.

"Hell no!" Malik shouted.

"She's on the other line and said you basically used her."

"You know your cousin better than me, but I've never lied to the women I've slept with."

"Okay...Well, let me call you back."

"I need you back here," Malik spoke up before I could disconnect with him.

I ran my hand through my hair in frustration.

"I'll have Reece get the plane ready," I said and ended the call before I turned to Reece.

Reece finished her call. "The plane is ready."

"Sarai, I can't promise I won't curse your cousin out when we get back," Arianna muttered, walking into the house. I didn't blame her because this whole mess was a big front that Asia was trying to put on to get ahead.

"This is interrupting my date...Ugh," Essence screeched.

"Sorry, boo, my brother needs me," Arianna stated in a soothing manner.

Half an hour later we drove off from the house toward the airstrip, and I looked back at the two story ten thousand square foot mansion thinking of the next time I'd be able to come and relax on my own. My cell phone vibrated. It was my assistant texting about Asia preparing to do another interview. I returned her text and said to send a cease and desist letter. Right before I closed out of my messages, a number popped up and I declined, figuring it was probably Christopher again.

"Reece, what can you tell me about Asia?"

"Honestly I never saw this coming," Reece told me.

"How bad can this get, Sarai?" Gabriella questioned.

I sighed, thinking of the time Arianna and Kash had a huge media crisis and it took me a few weeks to get things calmed down and cleared up. Asia was causing more problems than I ever expected.

"Very bad," I replied.

"I know she's your cousin, but she deserves to get her ass kicked," Arianna stated.

The car arrived at the airstrip and stopped. The driver opened the passenger doors for us, and we stepped out, heading up the stairs of the private plane.

"I don't believe I'd stop you." Asia's machinations were keeping me and my girls from having a bit of relaxation before the upcoming charity race. Not to mention, her accusations could possibly destroy Malik's reputation. We might not be friends per se, but no one deserved that and I would use everything in my arsenal to make sure she didn't succeed in tearing him down and hurting Pierce Motors' reputation.

"Call Cyrus and see what he thinks before you do anything rash," Reece said, taking a seat next to me on the plane.

"I hate to drag him into this mess."

"He's friends with Malik. Cyrus would want to help," Reece remarked, and I agreed, taking out my phone and dialing his number. He answered the call.

"I've spoken with Malik," Cyrus said, not even waiting for me to speak.

"Yeah, he called us and we're heading back now."

"I'll put in a few calls, I have some friends in the media," Cyrus explained.

"Okay. Thanks."

The seatbelt sign came on and the doors closed as we got comfortable preparing to fly back home.

"I'll contact Teddy about removing her from Cyrus Premier Enterprises until further notice," Reece said.

"Thanks, Reece. I'd prefer to not put you in the

middle of family problems, but she's gone too far this time."

"I know Malik and he'd never do anything like what she's claiming," Gabriella said.

"Yeah, I agree," Essence said.

\* \* \*

Once the flight landed, we dropped everyone off, then Reece and I drove to my place to talk with Malik and get the details of what happened. The town car stopped and we jumped out, grabbing our bags. Reece got a call from Cyrus that he was already with Malik so she wouldn't have to worry about getting a ride home. The doorman greeted us as flashes of light and photographers yelled as they jumped in front of us.

"Sarai Lambert, are you representing Malik Pierce?" a photographer asked.

"No comment," I said and moved around him, heading inside.

"I can see this getting bad, Sarai. Are you sure about this?" Reece asked as we stepped on the elevator. I held my purse on my shoulder and blew out a breath of frustration.

"It's my job, Reece. I have no choice."

# Chapter Thirteen

## Malik

I sipped the last bit of scotch in my glass, watching over the night lights and traffic coursing through the city while standing on my balcony. Cyrus continued talking on the phone to *Sports Channel News* about cutting an exclusive interview that Asia wanted to do. I should have fired her a long time ago and things wouldn't have gotten this far. My doorbell rang and I turned to head back inside. I chuckled as Cyrus started yelling at someone on the phone. I opened the door, seeing Sarai and Reece with their luggage. At first, I was worried about getting Sarai involved because it was her family and causing a rift between women was not something that I strived to do. But now, I'm glad she's on my side because she's damn good at her job.

"Thanks for coming," I said.

"My job is twenty-four-seven," Sarai said, walking inside pulling her luggage behind her. Reece leaned over and gave me a hug.

"How are you?" Reece asked.

"I'm good, just pissed that photographers are camping outside my office and home now," I stated.

"What happened exactly? I need all the details, so I'll know how to push forward," Sarai asked as she waved at Cyrus. He ended his call and Reece walked toward him, pecking his lips as he pulled her into a hug.

Finishing off my scotch, I set the glass down on the table.

"It happened at the office. She made a pass at me and I pushed her off me and fired her."

"What type of pass?" Sarai asked and pulled her phone out and started typing. Sitting down in the chair next to her I clasped my hands together and thought back to the day in my office.

*Two days ago.*

*"Kendra, go home, you've done enough," I said.*

*"Are you sure?" Kendra questioned.*

*"I'm positive, I'll be here for another hour and then I'm heading home."*

*"Okay, well make sure you get some rest. Canon sent over the marketing proofs."*

*"Great, anyone else left?" I asked.*

*"Asia and a few people in accounting."*

*"Tell her she can leave as well."*

*"Good, because she hasn't done anything at all that could be called work," Kendra blurted out.*

*"I know, send her in here because I'm done wasting my time."*

*"Okay, do you need me in on the conversation?" Kendra asked.*

*I shook my head, letting her know I'd be fine. Kendra waved bye and a few minutes later Asia swished inside, smiling from ear to ear.*

"I like working in the office at night. It's peaceful," Asia said, sitting on the edge of my desk.

"Asia—"

Asia held her finger on my lips to be quiet and my eyebrows furrowed in confusion. Before I could realize what was happening, she bent down and kissed me, and I jerked back in shock.

"What are you doing?" I questioned and jumped up.

"Doing what you've wanted me to do," Asia said.

"Didn't I say the first time that I'm not interested?"

"Please, Malik, you didn't mean it," Asia replied while she moved in closer. She ran a hand up my chest. I gripped her hands and pushed her back gently to put space between us.

"Asia, you seem to not understand but when a man says he's not interested, nine times out of ten he doesn't want you."

Asia removed her hands out of my hold and tried to reach her arms around my neck and I shoved her back again.

"Is it because of Sarai?" she asked.

"No. I'm not into young women that throw themselves at me."

She scoffed and planted her hands on her hips. "I'm giving you a chance to be with me and you're turning me down?"

"When did you become a prize for me?"

"I suggest you realize what's in front of you, we could be good for each other, Malik," Asia teased, grabbing my hand, and entwining our fingers.

I chortled at her determination and pointed between the both of us. "This will never happen. Pack your bags, you're fired."

*She gasped in shock; her face contorted in anger.*

*"You can't fire me!" she shouted.*

*"I can and I did," I said and sat back down to continue working.*

*"Malik, what's going on here?" Kendra asked, strolling inside.*

*Asia shifted from one foot to the other. "You put him up to this didn't you?" Asia spat.*

*"Excuse me?" Kendra snapped.*

*"Asia, leave before I call security."*

*"You'll regret this, Malik, I'm not to be played with," Asia stated before she stomped off, bumping Kendra on the shoulder as she left.*

Present day.

"Wow," Reece said.

"Now we're here."

"So, it's your word against hers," Cyrus spoke and I nodded.

"Yeah, Kendra came in at the end, but she knew I wanted to fire Asia a while back and I was giving her another chance before this situation," I said.

"The charity race is coming up, so we need to try to contain it as much as possible," Sarai said, reminding us all of what was at stake.

"I agree. Malik, you have too much on the line and All Hands Homes will end up getting dragged into the situation," Reece told me.

"Plus, Cyrus Premier Enterprises," Cyrus said.

"What has Jackson said?" Sarai questioned.

"He believes me and wants to continue with the race," I answered.

Sarai stood up and grabbed her bags. Reece and Cyrus followed behind gathering her things to leave.

"Let me get in the office and figure some things out. I would have a talk with Asia, but it might make things worse," Sarai stated.

"I was trying to avoid having to call you, but since you're the best in the business, I didn't have a choice."

"You did the right thing. Let me work my magic and I'll have her apologizing before it explodes further," Sarai said before she grasped my hand in comfort as she left my condo and headed toward her place.

"Malik, you have our full support at Cyrus Premier Enterprises. Pierce Motors is a long-time business partner and friend to us," Cyrus stated as he extended his hand. I shook hands with him and watched as he and Reece left for the night. I closed the door and headed to the couch and sat down, ran a hand over my face. I picked up the Kessler whiskey and poured another shot. Swishing the liquid around, I took the shot, closed my eyes, and let the smooth, warm taste flow into my system.

"Welcome to being VP of a major corporation," I muttered to myself.

* * *

The next day in front of my office building a large crowd of paparazzi and news organizations were camped out front. I got out of my car and pushed through the crowd.

"Is it true, Malik? You fired Asia Lambert because she turned you down?" a reporter asked me.

"No comment," I replied.

"We have an exclusive statement from Asia Lambert," a reporter from *Celebrity Style* blogger yelled out.

"Good for you," I told her, and explained to the front security to call the police and get them removed.

I stepped on the elevator to head to my office to try and get some work done. Before the doors closed, Canon held his hand out to stop the doors from closing then stepped inside.

"Bro, it's crazy out front," Canon said.

"I know. Sarai said she was taking care of it."

"Have you talked to Asia since it happened?" he questioned.

"No. I called my lawyer for a restraining order."

"That's good," Canon said, following me out of the elevator and down the hallway toward my office.

"Any messages, Kendra?" I asked as I stopped at her desk.

"Yes, some news reporters and magazines. Plus, the clothing distributor wants to talk," Kendra mentioned, and I grimaced. If Asia messed up a business opportunity for my company, I'd more than likely be ready to bury her where she stood.

"Get our lawyers for Pierce Motors on the line, I want to make sure they can't end the contract over this situation." I picked up the cup of coffee she pointed at with my name on top.

I opened my office door, placed my coffee and briefcase down on my desk, then pulled off my jacket.

"Do you need me in the meeting?" Kendra questioned, standing in the archway of the door.

"No, make sure we're all set with my tux for the charity dinner."

"Gotcha boss," Kendra said.

"All right, talk to me. How are things going?" I asked.

"Are you sure you're ready to work? I mean you have a lot going on, bro," Canon said.

"I need to stay busy while I can."

"Who are you taking to the charity dinner?" Canon inquired.

"Nobody."

"You should take someone, it might help get them off your back with the whole Asia situation," Canon told me.

I scratched the back of my neck. "I'll think about it, maybe ask Arianna if she has any single and sane friends."

"What about Alyssa?" Canon asked.

"Hell no! She's too co-dependent and controlling and after all the months of us just kicking it together as friends, now she wants something serious."

"I'm glad to be married and not have your problems," Canon joked. I flipped him off and opened the drawer of my desk and picked up my notepad.

"Fuck you, Canon. All right, so how many pieces will we have?"

"According to the designer, they launched with a hundred pieces, and their marketing budget went over twenty-five thousand dollars," Canon stated.

"Check with Cyrus and see if we can get Kamden to be featured in our campaign."

"That'll be a cool crossover with Cyrus Premier Enterprises."

"Yep, and do a photoshoot at the tracks."

"You know that will send the budget over, adding another photoshoot?" Canon inquired.

"The way they have my name in the mud, we need to do something to put the focus back on the work of Pierce Motors."

"Sounds good, let me get out of here and try to plan some more space for marketing," Canon explained.

"Thanks, Canon." As soon as Canon walked out of my office, my office phone rang.

"Hey, glad I caught you," Sarai said over the phone. I leaned back in my seat, listening to her speak.

"Is that directed to me or the person next to you?" I challenged.

"Sorry, I'm in my office talking with my assistant," Sarai stated.

"Hopefully it's about my case."

"It's about your case and mine actually."

"What's going on with you?" I sat up straight at the strain in her voice.

"You're not the only one dealing with someone that can't take no for an answer."

"What are you doing for lunch today?" I asked.

"Nothing, I have calls to return and emails to send out," Sarai explained.

"Have lunch with me."

"That's not a good idea."

"Lunch between a client and a publicist is always a good idea."

"We shouldn't," Sarai insisted.

"Lunch to discuss your plans on Asia and the charity race is good. I'll see you at noon," I said, and she finally agreed, ending the call. I closed out of the computer and made a call to get one of my favorite restaurants to deliver wraps and drinks.

# Chapter Fourteen

## Malik

The wraps were warm and spicy. Sarai was sitting next to me on the couch in my office laughing at Kendra from her dancing in joy for having the Philly steak and cheese wrap.

"She's hilarious," Sarai said.

"Kendra's a trip."

"I like her," Sarai mentioned.

"Don't tell her, but I like her too. She's grown on me over the years."

Sarai chuckled and bit into her wrap. She was wearing a purple sleeveless dress with her hair hanging down with a part in the middle and minimal makeup.

"I have my own version of Kendra. My assistant Selena is just as funny."

"What made you want to get into this type of business, Sarai? To push bad media attention on you?" I questioned.

"I kind of love figuring out other people's problems. It's easier for me than dealing with my own," Sarai said, taking a sip of her bottle of water.

"Your ex is one of your problems?" I wondered.

"Not anymore, he cheated, and I broke up with him almost seven months ago," Sarai said.

I popped a french fry in my mouth.

"What about you and relationships?" Sarai questioned me.

"I don't do relationships, women are too complicated."

Sarai laughed at my statement.

"In regard to your current predicament, I can see your objections. But they can be beautiful if you had the right person," Sarai said as she peered into my eyes.

"Tell me about Sarai Lambert."

"Not much to say besides I built my business on my own, I'm single, my parents didn't last, and I was raised by a single mother," Sarai explained.

"You don't sound as enthusiastic about your mother."

Sarai scooted back on the couch. "Our relationship can be a little aggravating at times."

"Pressure."

"Huh?"

"Having pressure from family to be something that you don't necessarily want to be, but they've sacrificed so you feel obligated."

"Pressure," Sarai repeated.

I sat back on the couch with my arm stretched out across the back. I licked my lips and moved my eyes from Sarai's legs up to her pouty lips.

"Pressure?" Sarai asked.

"Huh?"

"Do you feel pressure to kiss me?"

"A part of me wants to and the other part is saying this could be a mistake."

"Same," Sarai said and leaned over. I gripped her chin and she brushed her lips against mine. I caressed my tongue across her bottom lip, biting it slowly, and pulled it between my lips. A sweet, low moan escaped her. Sarai planted her hands against my chest, and I laid further down on the couch with her on top of me.

"Mmmm...Malik," Sarai whispered. I gripped her waist, running a hand down her back across her ass.

"I know," I mumbled.

A knock on the door surprised us both as Kendra walked inside without waiting. We jumped apart, putting distance between us.

"Ohhh...did I interrupt something?" Kendra asked. Sarai cleared her throat, wiping her lips with the napkin, then passed one for me to get the lipstick off my face.

"What's up, Kendra?" I asked, standing up.

"I wanted to tell Sarai that *Celebrity Style* magazine retracted Asia's statement," Kendra said.

"Thanks, Kendra," Sarai replied, gathering up her trash.

Kendra strolled out of the office and I watched Sarai prepare to leave.

"I'll see you at the charity dinner," Sarai announced as she picked up her purse and keys.

Not ready for her to leave I stepped in front of her and lifted her chin, reaching out to take her hands in mine.

"Be my date."

"Whattt..." Sarai stuttered.

"For the charity dinner. Allow me to escort you down the red carpet."

"Like an actual date?" Sarai remarked.

"Listen, both of us know there's something between us that we need to explore."

"Malik, I never get involved with my clients," Sarai confessed.

"Too late," I said, then bent down, slid my hand around the back of her neck, and captured her lips again. Sarai gripped my suit jacket and deepened the kiss as I parted her lips with my tongue. I groaned, feeling her hands run up and down my back. This strong pull between us caused my dick to jump in my pants. Sarai stepped away and I had a sly smirk on my face when I ran my thumb across her lips.

"Be ready at seven," I said, and she nodded in answer.

* * *

*Charity race: one week later.*

I hadn't seen Sarai since that day in my office. Either I was busy with work or she was slammed with getting Asia to retract her statements. Sarai and I talked on the phone a few times, discussed what plans I had for our date tonight and what she liked to do outside of working. She showed me some of the pictures from the girls trip that had been cut short because of Asia blasting me in the media.

Speaking of Asia, Sarai's mother was sticking up for her. She made it seem as though Sarai interfered in a relationship that Asia and I had. Something that was a straight up lie since I'd never even wanted Asia in my office, let alone a relationship.

At least, until Sarai. I knew she was leery about us because of her ex and his cheating. I'd planned on talking with Cyrus to get advice on dating a woman who continued to challenge you at every step.

Asia texted me a few times and tried to apologize. I ended up blocking her and let my lawyer handle any communication. My parents and Jackson were happy that things were finally clearing up and the plans for me to be announced as CEO were supposed to happen tonight. I came in early to make sure security was tight and all the cars were cleared for inspection. I left my office and walked around with security, making sure things were flowing easily for the charity race.

This was the highest profile event every year for Pierce Motors and Cyrus Premier Enterprises and it brought in a lot of sponsors, industry celebrities, and coverage for us internationally. I waved at my niece and nephew sitting in the crowd with my mom. Jackson and my dad were talking to reporters, Tripp was laughing and talking with Kash. I had security following behind Arianna while she did interviews today. Signs posted around the venue and out front announced our new clothing line. We even had some celebrities and musicians come out and sit in the VIP stands.

"How's it looking?" Cyrus asked after he finished his interview.

We shook hands and I patted him on the shoulder.

"Things are great. I'm ready to get it over with and get the dinner going." Cyrus followed me over to the pit crew.

"Sarai's really agreed to be your date tonight?" he questioned.

"You sound shocked," I replied, slapping hands with Tripp and Brody.

"It's Sarai Lambert," Cyrus joked. All of the guys laughed at Cyrus, and I waved him off.

"Whatever, man."

Cyrus put his hands up, backing down.

"Mr. Pierce, we're ready to start," Kendra said as she walked back over to the stands. The announcement started, and reporters moved away from the center pit as cars started to line up. Seeing the blood, sweat, and ideas pay off with the amount of coverage we'd have afterwards made it worth it, along with the launch of our clothing line.

"*Ladies and gentlemen please stand for the national anthem!*" the announcer said.

A few minutes later the crowd clapped hands and the countdown began. The cameras zoomed in and the cars took off around the track while everyone cheered and screamed for Kamden and Arianna. A few more upcoming drivers received some love, but the main event was watching Kamden reign supreme at the racetrack. I walked over to the stands to check in with my family. Reece, Essence, and Gabriella were sitting together. I bent down and hugged Mom and Cicely.

"Y'all having fun?" I asked, and they smiled as I kissed their cheeks.

"Malik, we saw the venue decorations for tonight. Everything is perfect," Reece explained.

"That's good to know, Reece. Have you seen Sarai?" I asked.

"She was still running through the venue to make sure everyone was prepared," Reece told me.

"Okay, I'll send her a text to make sure we're on time," I said and checked my watch. Charity events didn't last long so we'd be done in the next twenty minutes. Then we'd prepare everyone to board the busses and head to the venue.

"I told her to be ready by seven," I explained as I looked over at the cars pulling into the garage pits.

Madison ran over to me.

"Uncle Malik, can I ride with you?" Madison tapped me on the leg so I picked her and kissed her cheek.

"I can't, princess. I have work to do, but I'll see you at dinner."

Madison rolled her eyes, smiled, and pinched my cheek. "Okay. Do you have a dollar?" She held her hand out and I grimaced at her question.

"Are you trying to play me like your brother?"

"I would never." Madison winked her left eye at her brother right in front of my face.

I put her back down on her feet and slipped a hand into my pocket and pulled out my wallet, giving her a dollar.

"That's it?" Madison scoffed as she turned the money front to back like it would magically change. Everybody in the stands laughed at us and I bent down and kissed her cheek again.

"You are too spoiled."

Madison walked back over to her parents.

"All right let me get going and I'll see you in a few minutes," I told my family and friends. I headed out of the stands and shook hands with a few sponsors that Jackson had introduced me to. A few reporters asked for an interview and I passed, not wanting to be the center of attention, and allowed Arianna and Kash to take over while I left to go meet with Sarai for our date.

* * *

An hour later I pulled up to the same venue that Enterprises used for their auction bids. Cyrus and Reece talked me into holding it there since it brought out so many bigwigs for them the first time.

I checked my tie and stepped out of my Mercedes Benz and handed the key to the valet. The crowd of reporters was huge and I saw Sarai up front talking with a few of them. Seeing the way she looked had me wanting to skip the entire event and go out to dinner just the two of us. The lights flashed on the red carpet, celebrities mixed and mingled as they walked down the carpet and posed. Some were athletes and celebrities I'd been a big fan of since I was a young kid. I stepped on the red carpet right as they called my name to turn left and right. It was overwhelming and annoying to keep up with every voice yelling out your name.

*"Malik! Malik! Over here," reporters shouted.*

*"Malik, to the right!" another photographer screamed.*

I was tired of the noise. I started to move along the press line when Sarai noticed me and headed toward me. I locked our hands and the cameras created a frenzy I wasn't expecting. I leaned over and whispered in her ear.

"You look beautiful."

Sarai smiled and mouthed thank you, then pointed at Arianna and Kash taking photos. I peered up and saw the rest of my family coming up behind them.

I gripped her hand and placed my hand on the small of her back.

"Let's head inside."

I admired her sexy curves in the blue dress that hugged every inch and caught her scent; she smelled light and floral.

"What's the perfume you're wearing?" I opened the

door to let us inside the building where the large entrance was decorated with Pierce Motors and Cyrus Premier Enterprises posters. All Hands Homes large name was flashed over the big screen. Jackson and his wife, Emery, came our direction.

"Malik, great job, it's looking good in there." Jackson reached out for a handshake.

"Thanks, but I can't take all the credit. Sarai and Reece did most of the work." Emery hugged Sarai and I was surprised they knew each other already.

"How do you two know each other?"

"We met through Arianna," Emery stated.

"How are the kids, Emery?"

"Running us crazy as usual, remind me why I had four kids and a big kid named Jackson," Emery fussed as she pointed at Jackson. I busted out in laughter and Jackson hugged Emery around the waist and pecked her lips.

"I'm not getting involved in that."

Cyrus and Reece ran over and they had harsh glares on their faces.

"We need to talk." Cyrus didn't let me reply as he planted his hand on my shoulder.

"What's going on?" I slipped my hands in my pockets.

"A few reporters are yelling at Arianna about cheating because you set it up for her to win last year," Cyrus explained as I stepped back in shock and crossed my arms over my chest.

"What reporter and exactly what did they say?" Sarai pulled up her dress so she wouldn't fall and started walking back out to the crowd.

"Kamden is about to punch a paparazzi in his face. Malik, you need to do something," Reece stated.

"Show me."

Cyrus and Reece headed back outside, Jackson and Emery started to follow and I stopped them.

"Jackson, it would probably be better if you kept things running inside and I'll handle the outside with Sarai."

"Are you sure?" Jackson wondered as he pulled his ringing phone out of his pocket and his face went hard.

"Hello," Jackson said.

"Let's go."

We started to head out again when Jackson called my name.

"We got a problem, Malik," Jackson said and put his phone on speaker.

"Who is that?"

"Hey, Malik, it's Jameson. I just got an email from the Racing Commission that an anonymous tip said you guys cheated last year and you're now under investigation," Jameson spoke.

"That's bullshit!" I shouted, pacing back and forth.

"I know, but we need to get to the bottom of this before it really gains traction," Jameson said.

# Chapter Fifteen

## Malik

Sarai tried to calm me down and I yanked out of her hold and walked toward the reporters.

"That's a lie!" Arianna screamed.

The photographer shrugged his shoulders and continued taking pictures of Arianna while yelling out *cheater*.

"Keep lying on my wife and see what happens," Kamden announced.

"Arianna, stop talking and let me handle this."

"Mr. Pierce, are you ready to explain how you won last year when most of your drivers were barely making the cut?" a reporter from *Sports Channel* inquired, pushing the microphone in my face.

"We don't cheat, and our drivers are the best because they work hard."

"A tip said you've been paying off someone to keep your secrets," the reporter announced.

"Who in their right mind would think I cheated?"

Security came around to try and stop Kash from hitting the photographer.

"Alyssa. Does that name sound familiar?" the *Sports Channel* reporter challenged, and my eyes bucked wide open in surprise that Alyssa would stoop to this level to try and get me back.

"No comment, and if you have any more questions, call my office," Sarai announced then motioned for us to move into the building.

"I need to go."

"Where? To talk to Alyssa?" Sarai questioned as she planted her hands on her hips.

"Malik, meet me in the office." Jackson grabbed Emery's palm, walking off.

"What are you thinking?" Cyrus wondered.

"You don't think we cheated, do you?"

"No, of course not, and Kamden wouldn't be the first person I'd think of doing anything like that if someone got accused," Cyrus remarked while he wrapped his arm around Reece's shoulders and pulled her in close.

"Malik, we didn't cheat and whatever Alyssa is talking about is a lie," Arianna spoke up, hugging close to Kamden.

I licked my lips, ready to get out of there and have a drink to clear my head. Sarai was still staring at me, waiting for an answer, and I wondered if she believed the lies, especially after the Asia situation.

"Cyrus, I'll call you later. Let me get out of here." I slid my valet ticket out of my pocket and walked off as Sarai called out behind me. A few minutes later my car was brought up front and I hopped inside. Before I could drive off Sarai jumped in the passenger side.

"What are you doing?" I sighed and leaned back in my seat then ran a hand down my face in frustration.

"I'm going with you." Sarai grabbed her seatbelt and locked the door.

"I was planning on being alone, can't promise I'll be good company," I said as I slid the key in the ignition.

"I didn't ask you to be good."

Taking out my phone messaged my brother. Jackson would understand, once I cleared my head we could talk. I dropped my phone back in my pocket and headed onto the main road.

* * *

I texted Cyrus and told him I'd call him in the morning, then drove to my beach house, which was near his place on Baker Road. Dealing with the cheating scandal of Pierce Motors and Asia's accusations at the same time was too much and I needed to shut the world out and figure out my next move. Jackson was pissed his company was being dragged through the mud and I wouldn't put it past him to want me to step aside until things cleared up.

Glancing over at Sarai, enjoying the way she wore the light blue ruffled dress that stopped just below her knees. Surprisingly, she sat quietly in the car while I drove, which I appreciated because when I got in one of my moods, I needed peace and quiet to think. My next move would be figuring out how I could have gotten two women to lie about me in the span of a few months.

I had a feeling Asia was behind it all and it wasn't just Alyssa talking to some random gossip blog on her own.

Sitting outside on the upper deck of my private beach, the moonlight shone down while a cool breeze whipped up the waves that gently drenched the sand. I took a sip of the warm scotch while still wearing my tuxedo shirt and pants. I had ripped my jacket off once we got inside.

Before I heard the door open fully, I could smell her sweet floral scent float through the air. "You shouldn't have come." I usually don't smoke cigars, but when I'm deep in thought I pull one out and sit here watching the waves. I stared over to see her walk up with a blanket around her arms.

"There you go trying to boss me around again."

I smirked, tilted the glass toward her, and guzzled the rest down. Sarai sat on the edge of my lounge chair and crossed her legs.

"Do you believe them?" I asked.

"Who?"

"The reporters, bloggers, and all of America I guess." I ran a hand up her back to keep her warm.

"No. You're a lot of things, Malik, but a cheater isn't one of them," Sarai stated and I chuckled.

"I like to come up here and relax—away from all the bullshit. My little getaway," I confessed.

"You have a beautiful home."

"You looked beautiful tonight."

"Thank you."

"So, Christopher and you?" I questioned.

"My ex-boyfriend," Sarai said, rubbing up and down her arms. I put my glass down and leaned over to pull her in between my legs with her back facing me to help keep her warm.

"You cold?" I asked.

"A little."

"Tell me about your ex."

"He was my life at one point, and I gave too much up believing he loved me the way I loved him. Same old

124

story, eventually, I caught him cheating," Sarai answered. My left hand entwined together with hers, my right hand sliding across her stomach as I rubbed in small circles.

"He's a fool," I said.

"What about you and Alyssa?"

I leaned my head back on the deck chair.

"She was someone that I could call on that didn't expect commitment."

"Are you sure about that? Because the link is saying the story is coming from a woman," Sarai told me.

"Alyssa wouldn't cause me all these problems because I ended things."

Sarai tried to get up and I tightened my hold on her stomach.

"I like you right here in this spot," I said.

"I can't imagine why," Sarai tittered.

I pinched her gently on the thigh.

"Are you still hung up on your ex?" I questioned.

"No, it's been over for months, he still tries to call, and I block him," Sarai stated.

"You know me and Asia never did anything, right? She tried and I told her straight up I wasn't interested," I explained. Sarai leaned up and turned toward me.

"You don't need to explain it to me, Malik. Asia's always gone for the guy that could buy her a lifestyle and you turned her down, so she's pissed."

"What about you?" I asked as I gripped her chin gently and ran a finger up and down her cheek.

"I don't know anymore. Somehow, I keep ending up with a broken heart."

"Do you think it's a good idea to be here with me? You know the paparazzi are probably hanging out in front of my place waiting to get a shot of you."

"I keep telling myself I shouldn't have come."

"Is that what you want? To leave and forget this night ever happened?" I asked. Sarai shook her head no and bit her bottom lip. A second passed before I felt her small hand move up my chest as she leaned in to capture my lips.

"Mhmmm..." she moaned, and I let my hand roam down her arm and across her back, pulling her close to my chest. Gripping both ass cheeks I was trying my best to think of something else before I exploded. I didn't have any expectations for tonight, and I was letting her run the show, because the last thing I needed was her regretting what happened. I pulled back and lowered my lips to her ear, biting and sucking gently behind her ear.

"You're fucking sexy as hell, Sarai," I confessed.

"Show me," Sarai replied.

I groaned and pulled back, peering into her eyes.

"Are you sure? The minute I slide in between your sweet thighs, I don't want you regretting anything."

"Shut up, Malik, and fuck me."

"Is this bossy Sarai talking now?"

She slid her hand across my hard erection and squeezed.

"Last time to change your mind, Rai," I said, giving her a nickname.

"Kiss me." Sarai leaned over and sucked my tongue into her mouth, slipping her palm under my shirt, and rubbed up my chest then down to my pants, unbuckling them.

I pulled back. "Take this dress off." Sarai turned around so I could unzip the back of her dress and she stepped out of it only wearing a black thong and one of those strapless bras. She took my breath away with how gorgeous she looked in the light of the moon. I lifted her palm then planted a kiss on her hand.

"Are you sure about this, Sarai? I can't promise I'll be slow and sweet with you."

Sarai put her left foot on the outside of my chair and sat down in my lap, with her legs wide open for me to see the full view of her sweet mound.

"I never asked you to be sweet with me, Malik."

I lifted my shirt off and tossed it on the ground and wrapped my hands around Sarai's waist, pulled her in close, smelled her sweet perfume, and kissed across her shoulder and up to her lips.

"Shit...you smell good."

"Mmmmm...Malik," Sarai moaned, gripping my dick.

I pushed her back gently and told her to lie down, then I ripped her thong off and swiped my tongue across her mound. My gaze dropped from her eyes to her shoulders then to her breasts and I squeezed and pulled the cup down, teasing her left nipple. I used my index finger and tweaked each nipple.

"Ahhhh....Malik," Sarai cried out as she dug her nails into my hand.

A shudder passed through her when my tongue entered her sweet pussy.

"Ohhh...baby." Sarai shook her head back and forth.

She arched, moaned, and shifted her leg up around my neck. With a groan I slipped my hands around to lift her ass off the chair, sucking up all of her juices.

"Fuck!" Sarai screamed as she gripped the back of my head while I stroked her bundle of nerves with my thumb.

# Chapter Sixteen

## Malik

I grabbed the condom out of my wallet before pants fell to the floor, and watched as Sarai rolled it down my hard erection. I slid inside of her. She was tight and wet, and I knew she could feel every inch of me. I pulled out slowly and tapped my dick against her lower lips. Wanting another taste of her, I shifted and picked her up by her ass, lifted her up on my shoulders, and she screamed when I slowly walked us back into the house while eating her pussy standing up, then stopped against the wall.

"Malik!... Don't... Oh my god!" Sarai screamed loudly.

"Don't move," I demanded and squeezed her body tight as my tongue buried into the swollen folds of her flesh. I couldn't resist her any longer. I drank in her intoxicating taste as she writhed against me. We made it to my bedroom and I placed her on the bed, staring at her sexy, sweet body.

"Damn."

Sarai's chest heaved up and down.

"I can't feel my legs," Sarai mentioned, and I chuckled, leaning against the bed and crawling over her body to line my dick up with her entrance.

"I'm just getting started, baby." I eased back inside and glided a palm across her abdomen, wanting to touch every curve of her body as I thrust inside. I bent down and kissed her lips. She pulled away and nuzzled her face in my neck, nipping her teeth on my veins. She matched my strokes as her moans grew louder.

"Ughhh...God, Malik."

"Shit, Sarai!"

Sarai gasped, grabbing the sheets tight as her climax hit. I watched her facial expressions as she shook in my arms and I came right behind her and fell down next to her on the bed out of breath, then pulled her against me, kissing the side of her face.

"How do you feel?" Sarai ran her thumb against my bottom lip. I stuck my tongue out and bit it and she giggled as I turned us over with me hovering over her body again. I kissed her once, twice and stood up to grab another condom out of my drawer next to the couch in my bedroom.

"I feel like I was hit by a truck. At the same time, I'm glad you're here with me."

Sarai reached up and touched my face, leaned up, and kissed my lips.

We continued having sex throughout the night until early in the morning. I'd never felt a connection with someone the way I did tonight with Sarai.

\* \* \*

Two days later, I was sitting in my office with Jackson, Cyrus, and Sarai, watching the news breaking of our company being dragged through the mud. I felt Sarai's hand on my thigh, trying to calm me down.

"What are the chances Asia put this in Alyssa's ear?" Cyrus asked as he turned toward me, and I tapped the pen against the table. Kendra was sitting at the end of the conference table taking notes.

"I'll find out. I think money is the motive, especially since Asia put out that little statement apologizing for lying," Sarai said.

"Do you want me to step down, Jackson?" I asked, waiting to hear the bad news. I hadn't taken anyone's calls or talked to my family. It took a while for me to understand this was part of being in a high-profile family, and people were always trying to bring us down.

"I'm not going to lie, I did tell Jameson to take your name off as CEO," Jackson stated, and Kendra gasped in shock. "But after talking with Emery and Uncle Eddison, I'm going to stick with you," Jackson said.

"Are you sure? Because the second Sarai does this, we can't take it back."

"You have the full backing of the company, Malik. Do what you need to do," Jackson said and stood up, extending a hand for me to shake.

"Thanks, Jackson."

He nodded and Cyrus sat back in his seat grinning.

"This is going to be fun." Cyrus planted his feet on top of the conference desk, hands behind his hand.

"Now it's my turn to turn into the Sarai they don't want to see," Sarai mentioned and stood up to leave. I grasped her hand before she could walk out and leaned over to kiss her, not caring that it was in front of everyone.

Sarai wiped the residue of her lipstick off my lips and I smirked and watched her swish out of the office. I checked my suit jacket again and licked my lips thinking about having her ride my dick again before the day was over.

"Cyrus, are we set for the press conference at Cyrus Premier Enterprises?" I asked.

Cyrus stood and headed to the door, following me out of the conference room with Kendra chuckling.

"What's funny?"

"You two aren't slick and Cyrus, did you know about them?" Kendra queried.

"A man never kisses and tells," Cyrus joked.

He chuckled to himself.

"We have it set up at eleven a.m.," Cyrus said, answering my previous questions while popping a mint in his mouth.

"Great, as soon as Sarai gives the go ahead, we'll be ready to go." I read over my speech that Sarai wrote up for me. The past two days while I stayed at the beach house, Sarai went around the media circuit to get Alyssa discredited and Asia placed on gag order. I had plans to go to my parents house for dinner tonight since I stayed away so photographers wouldn't hound them. All of social media was dragging our name talking about cancel culture and buying people's silence.

"Kamden just texted and said Arianna will be there," Cyrus said.

"She needs to stay home; I can tell the stress it's put on her."

"The clothing launch is going well?" Cyrus asked, changing subjects.

"Yeah, and our distribution was increased from what Canon said."

"I can't tell you what to do, I'm the last person to talk about causing media attention," Cyrus said.

"Reece told me about how you wouldn't even care what they say." I grabbed my coat and keys.

"Let me get out of here. I have a practice with Brody," Cyrus said.

"Cool, let me get this interview over with and I can head home." Kendra picked up her purse and jacket since she was joining me at the track. Cyrus went in the opposite direction and got in his car. I jumped into my Range Rover and Kendra got in on the other side.

Sarai texted me as I started the ignition.

*Baby: Hey I spoke with Alyssa's lawyer.*

*Me: What did they say?*

*Baby: She won't reveal where she got the information.*

*Me: That's cool, get Jameson to draw up a lawsuit.*

*Baby: Sounds good.*

I closed out of my messages and pulled out of the building through the crowd of reporters.

I turned at the light and got behind Cyrus so we could head back to Cyrus Premier Enterprises. Sarai tried to play nice with Alyssa but she wanted to stick to her guns with this lie.

Now the plan was to draw up a defamation lawsuit. I'd have her wrapped up in a civil lawsuit for so long that it wouldn't matter if she was lying or not because I'd take her for every penny she had. Alyssa had already lost her job because of this stupid shit.

"You seem happier," Kendra said, pushing the mirror up.

"Please don't start that marriage talk. Sarai and I are just hanging out and enjoying each other's company."

"So, if she's dating other people, that's okay?" Kendra asked.

I gripped the steering wheel a little tighter at the mention of Sarai dating someone else.

Changing the subject, I asked, "Did you go through all of the accounts that Asia worked on?" I stopped at the light as Cyrus zoomed through right before it turned red. Kendra was in charge of making sure Asia didn't take anything or make any waves with the few clients she handled for Pierce Motors.

"Nice change of subject." Kendra popped a piece of gum in her mouth as I pulled off and continued following Cyrus. We arrived at Cyrus Premier Enterprises and I parked in the VIP reserved spot next to him and jumped out of the car. A van for *Sports Channel* was already here.

"Thanks, now focus on your job and less on my love life."

"If only your love life didn't interfere with my job," Kendra said sarcastically as I held the door open for her to walk inside.

"Malik, are you sure doing this press statement will help? We know we didn't cheat." Arianna walked over and hugged me.

"I can handle it, Ari. I'm not as smooth as Kash, but I'll get it done."

Everyone lined up as I left the main office and went over to the track. *Sports Channel* reporters were standing next to the podium.

"Mr. Pierce, are you ready?" Linda, the lead reporter at the station, asked.

"Yeah, let's get this over with."

"All right, I'll ask you a few questions and then we'll be done," Linda said before she motioned for the photographers to get ready. Kash and Arianna stood next to me, while Cyrus and Kendra stood off to the other side watching. I slid my hands into my pockets and stood behind the podium with the multiple microphones angled in front of my face.

"Mr. Pierce, we're here because you were accused of cheating to win a race last year," Linda stated.

Linda was the type that loved to get you stuck so you'd fumble when she was interviewing you. It was what they liked to call "gotcha" questions. Sarai mentioned they'd try this tactic if she wasn't around and I wasn't prepared to handle everything they threw at me.

"I can unequivocally say we did not cheat."

"We have witnesses that say otherwise," Linda said.

"They're lying. Pierce Motors is a family-owned business, started by my cousin. We've put in too much work to be labeled as a company that cheats."

"Alyssa stated that you told your sister Arianna to lie about the underweight."

"Anyone that knows Arianna will tell you that never happened. Alyssa is bitter and she lied."

"Has the president of the organization done an inspection of your vehicle?" Linda questioned.

"As soon as this lie was told we had the car checked and nothing was found. Also, Cyrus of Cyrus Premier Enterprises, the company we drove against, was there when this happened and nothing was found."

"Mr. Davidson, how do you feel about the allegations?" Linda pointed her microphone and turned the camera toward him.

"Malik and I are not only rivals on the track, but

friends off it, and I know this was just a money grab," Cyrus explained.

"Any more questions you have can be taken up with our lawyer. Thank you," I said and walked off as reporters continued talking into the cameras.

Cyrus and I went into the pit garage where Kamden's car was sitting.

"Are you racing today?" I asked him.

"Taking today off to spend it with Ari and little Kash," Kamden told me as he pulled Arianna to his side.

"You guys coming to family dinner?" I asked.

"Possibly, depends on how I feel later today," Ari said, rubbing her stomach. My little sister was having another baby and, as the middle child, I was still the only one without kids. I felt my phone vibrate and grabbed it out of my pocket.

*Baby: How did it go?*

*Me: I think I made an impression.*

*Baby: That doesn't sound good.*

*Me: What are you wearing?*

*Baby: How can you think about that at this time?*

*Me: Shit. It's been more than twenty-four hours since I was inside of you.*

*Baby: Well, you'll have to wait a little bit longer, I'm staying at home this week.*

I frowned at her statement about staying at her place tonight, since she'd been sleeping over at my place ever since we slept together. I found myself not being able to sleep at night without her next to me.

*Me: Why?*

*Baby: Don't start and have fun with your family tonight.*

I closed out the messages, slipping my phone inside

my coat pocket. I would drop Kendra off at the office and go check on Alyssa for starting this bullshit.

"I need to head out, I'll see you later, sis." I kissed Arianna's forehead and dapped Kamden, then Cyrus. Kendra hugged Arianna and Kamden goodbye, as I walked out to start the car.

We headed across town to where Alyssa stayed. Cyrus had gotten her address for me and I decided, as a last-ditch effort, to talk with her face to face and try to get her to retract the lies she'd put out to the public.

I turned onto the freeway and looked at the time. It was going on noon and then I had to get back to the office and work before dinner tonight.

"Kendra, I was going to drop you back at the office, but I won't make it in time."

"Where are you going?"

"You promise to stay in the car?"

"No," Kendra informed me and stared at the side of my face. I felt her eyes glaring at me in question.

"Alyssa's."

"Malik, you can't be serious."

"I am and you need to stay in the car."

"Huh... okay," Kendra muttered, but I didn't believe her at all.

We pulled up to Alyssa's apartment building in a Rochester neighborhood that wasn't too far from Pierce Motors. I cut the car off and jumped out, leaving the keys inside.

"I'm giving you five minutes, after that I'm coming in to get you," Kendra spat.

"I won't be long."

"You say that now, but we know when you get around

a pretty woman something takes over and you end up sleeping with her. No thanks if I don't believe you."

I shook my head at her statement and shut the driver's side door. I looked around the neighborhood and checked the time. I stepped up to the door and knocked. A few minutes later I heard the locks turning and Alyssa opened the door wearing only a robe that barely covered herself.

"Malik, what are you doing here?"

"We need to talk."

"This isn't a good time," Alyssa spat.

"Funny because you've tried for the last few months to talk."

# Chapter Seventeen

## Malik

Alyssa stepped to the side and allowed me to come inside. I glanced around seeing boxes, disarray of clothes scattered around and it looked like she was packing up.

"What do you want?" Alyssa asked.

"Why are you doing this really?"

"Please, like you really care." Alyssa walked around her couch to sit down.

"I'm asking you now."

"You're here because of the way things are blowing up for you in the media," Alyssa spat before she grabbed the remote and turned the TV up loud.

"We both know this was not a serious thing. Is this really about you wanting a relationship or money?"

"Asia said you'd say that," Alyssa mentioned.

I chortled at the mention of Asia's name. I knew this wasn't solely on Alyssa to cause this mess.

"How did you two meet?"

"She saw me leaving your place the night I came over to see you."

"She played you, Alyssa. Did she tell you how she wanted to have a relationship with me too?"

I came around to sit down on the coffee table and picked up her palms, making eye contact.

"Alyssa, you know we never meant for things to go too far. I need you to do the right thing and retract your statement."

Alyssa smiled and stood up in front of me, opening her robe and showing off her one-piece lingerie, and rubbed her stomach.

"What are you going to do for me?" Alyssa questioned right as a hard knock was heard at the door. I would never sleep with a woman that's pregnant by someone else, she's desperate at this rate.

"Malik! Your five minutes is up," Kendra shouted.

"Who is that?" Alyssa asked and stomped over to the front door. I sighed, jumping up to stop Kendra from going off on Alyssa.

"I'm giving you one more chance to do the right thing. Once I leave here, I can't help you," I said and opened the door to Kendra with her hand up getting ready to knock again. I pushed Kendra behind me, and Alyssa scoffed and shut the door in our faces.

"Glad you didn't screw this up and sleep with her ass," Kendra joked.

"That wasn't five minutes."

"You're lucky I didn't call Sarai on you," Kendra fussed as we headed to work.

* * *

Later that evening, I was having dinner with my parents, brother, sister-in-law, and niece and nephew. Cicely told me that she was at Sarai's condo cooking dinner for her and asked if I wanted any leftovers. I told her no since Mom had cooked.

"What are the lawyers saying?" Dad asked.

I pushed the broccoli around on my plate, not really feeling hungry and annoyed that Sarai wouldn't be in my bed when I got home.

"Jameson is filing a lawsuit against them both."

"So, Asia and Alyssa are working together?" Mom inquired, taking a sip of her water.

"Yep, Alyssa all but confessed today."

"Uncle Malik, what's a cheat?" Major questioned.

"Major, where did you hear that from?" Gabriella wondered.

"At school the kids keep saying Uncle Malik and Auntie RiRi cheated," Major said. I was pissed that it was affecting my nephew at school.

"Little man, the Pierce family doesn't cheat." I rubbed a palm across his head.

"I know and that's why I punched Tommy in the stomach for lying," Major mentioned, and Gabriella gasped then dropped her fork.

"Major, we don't hit in this family," Eddison Jr. said.

"Major, I want you to apologize to him tomorrow," Mom told him, and he nodded in answer.

"Listen to me, Major, you don't have to stick up for me. It's my job to protect you," I said and extended a fist toward him for a dap, and he smiled as he bumped knuckles with me.

"I know Arianna is upset, she was crying all day when it was announced at the charity dinner," Dad said.

"I'm taking care of things and Sarai is working overtime to get to the bottom of it."

Going on ten at night, I helped my mom wash dishes as my brother and family had already left half since it was a school night. To hear that Major was fighting in school because of my mess really upset me. Life should be easier for him and he shouldn't have to defend me.

"You like her, don't you?" Mom spoke, bringing me out of my daze.

"Is it that obvious?"

"Very much so. All night you kept checking your phone," Mom replied.

"She's sleeping at her place tonight and I was pissed."

"You're getting attached, huh?"

"What do you know about being attached?" I challenged as I took the plate out of her hand and dried it off.

"I know that you deserve to be happy and sometimes you tend to push people away." Mom dried her hands then turned the faucet off and leaned up against the wall.

"Never really considered myself the husband type, women can be a little..."

She pointed her finger up at me to not say the wrong word.

"Complicated," I answered.

"Love can be a complicated and beautiful thing. Don't cut it off before you have the chance to see it grow," Mom said and kissed me on the cheek. She left the kitchen to leave me alone with my thoughts. Could Sarai and I have a real relationship without the drama that can come with the last name Pierce? My father walked inside with a glass of Hennessy in his hand and passed it to me.

"I thought you could use this," Dad said.

"Thanks."

"I know this position wasn't your first choice and you did it out of obligation."

"Pops, let's not bring up the past." We clinked glasses and took the drink down in one shot.

"I'm proud of you no matter what you do with your life." I shook hands with him and talked for another hour or so about life in general before I left for home.

# Chapter Eighteen

## Malik

The next day I was at a lunch meeting with a prospective sponsor. Remy Barnett was an old college friend of mine and we briefly went out once or twice, but our friendship meant more to us. She was the co-owner of a beauty bar and wanted to look into possibly sponsoring Ari with Pierce Motors. I decided to treat her to lunch at Sonny's and get a feel for what we could do together as business partners.

"Malik, you haven't changed one bit." Remy flashed a huge grin at me.

I picked up the water jug and poured some, refilling her cup. "I'm the same guy, just a little more refined."

"I can see that." Remy giggled and brushed her palm across my shoulder.

"So, tell me about your ideas. My assistant called and said you've been wanting to meet with me." I cut into my steak and took a bite.

"Well, I have to confess, it wasn't just for business reasons."

"What do you mean?"

"I wanted to see if you were single still." Her arms dropped to her sides. I rubbed the back of my neck nervously trying to figure out how to let her down easy.

"Hey, I didn't see you here. I was just picking up some to-go food," Sarai said as she stopped at our table. I started to stand up and kiss her cheek but she held her hand up for me to stop.

"You look busy, don't get up on account of me," Sarai said, looking between me and Remy.

"Remy and I are talking business about Pierce Motors."

"Hopefully more than business will get done today." A little cocky smirk appeared on Remy's face.

"I wouldn't put it past him," Sarai said and marched off. I jumped up to stop her from leaving and pushed her into the women's bathroom.

"Hey! This is the ladies room," a woman shouted, and I apologized.

"Your lunch is on me," I explained and locked the door when she left.

"What are you doing?" Sarai questioned.

"What are you doing acting jealous?" I responded.

"I wasn't jealous of little miss Barbie out there."

"Remy's an old friend and she owns a beauty bar."

"Okay," Sarai said and started to walk off, but I blocked her from leaving with my hand on the door.

"She just asked me if I was single before you walked up and before I could tell her I was seeing someone."

She hugged herself.

"So, this someone that you're seeing. Is she pretty?" Sarai asked as she wrapped a curl around her finger.

"Very pretty."

"Is she prettier than Barbie outside?"

"Really, Sarai?"

"Fine, let me out," Sarai spat.

An amused expression quirked up the side of her mouth as she studied me.

"You realize that I can only deal with one crazy woman at a time, right?" I asked and grabbed her around the waist, turning our positions with her back to the door.

"What, pray tell, are you talking about, Malik?"

I tapped her on the end of her nose. "This mouth of yours, those eyes, legs, sexy ass, and sweet—"

"Shushh..."

"What, there's nobody in here."

"I know, but you always have me ready to grab my vibrator whenever you talk about my sex."

I burst into laughter at her statement.

"So, you admit I keep you ready and hot."

A knock at the door interrupted us.

"Malik, are you in the ladies' room?" Remy asked.

I leaned down and pressed a kiss to Sarai's lips before she did something stupid.

"Mmmmm..." Sarai groaned as she dropped her food on the floor.

"You good?" I questioned.

"I need to reorder my food."

"Put the order in and I'll take care of it for you."

"Okay." Sarai pecked my lips again and bent down to grab her bag of food, throwing it in the trash. I watched as she checked herself out in the mirror and smiled back at me as I opened the door. Remy was looking behind Sarai, directly at me.

"Are you two dating?" Remy questioned.

Sarai turned and patted me on the chest and kissed

me on the lips in front of Remy and her eyes went wide with shock.

"Thanks again for lunch, Malik," Sarai remarked and walked out of the restroom.

"Sorry, you wanted to sponsor how much again?" I asked and she stomped off in a huff.

I shook my head in disbelief at her wasting my time.

"Women."

# Chapter Nineteen

## Sarai

*Three days later*

I was home wearing my usual sweat shorts and sports bra, working overtime to get my people all over social media to send out cease and desist notices about the lies that Asia and Alyssa were spreading. I tried to play nice, but they wanted the beast to come out and this was what I was good at doing. I had a meeting with Alyssa earlier and she basically blew me off, so now things would end up getting ugly for her when the lawsuit was filed and Jackson took her to court for lying. A knock sounded at my door and I stood up, checked the time, and saw it was going on eleven p.m. Cicely left two hours ago after making food for the rest of the weekend for me. I looked out of the peephole and saw Malik standing on the other side of the door, so I opened it.

"What are you—"

Before I could finish my sentence, Malik reached out to grab my face, pulled me into his chest, and kissed my lips. I grasped his shirt and he lifted me in his arms as I wrapped my legs around his waist.

Malik pulled back and stared into my eyes. "I missed you today."

"I missed you too."

He slid his tongue across my bottom lip and I lowered my hand to his pants to unbuckle my new favorite wakeup clock. Sex with Malik was the best I'd ever had. Sex with Christopher was great, but it was nothing like this. Malik paid attention to my needs and made sure I was satisfied and watched to see if I was fully sated.

Malik walked me to my couch and sat me down as he grabbed a condom out of his wallet. I removed my sports bra and kicked off my shorts, stroking his dick as he grew harder in my hand before licking the tip of his mushroom head.

"Sarai," Malik groaned, gripping the curve of my neck as I took him to the back of my throat. I moaned and moved up then down a little, fondling his balls and caressing his thighs.

"Mmmmm..." I moaned.

"Okay...that's enough."

I released him and giggled as he tore the condom open, put it on, and lined his dick up with my sex, then entered me slowly as he ran a hand up to grip my breasts.

"Shit, this is home," Malik moaned and hovered over my body, capturing my lips. His strokes picked up and the sounds of our moans were heard through the room. Malik pushed my legs wider as he went deeper and pulled my nipple in his mouth, hungrily sucking as I felt myself getting dizzy. I nuzzled my face on the couch, as every emotion and pleasure ran through my mind. This was supposed to be a one-time, fun type of friends-with-bene-fits situation, but as time went on my feelings started to get serious and I hadn't decided if I'd confess them to him or not.

"Oooohhhh... Fuck!"

"God damn, Sarai. Your pussy is addictive, baby." Malik huffed as he pulled out of me and flipped me over the couch with my ass in the air. He smacked my ass, slid his index finger inside my pussy along with his tongue slowly, as I tried to run away while he grabbed my waist and kept me in place.

"Malik, please," I pleaded, barely able to control my hoarse voice from crying out in ecstasy. He pulled away and reached around and stuck his fingers in my wetness, playing with my clit as he slowly pushed his dick into my pussy, strokes picked up. I felt him deep in my cervix as my body shook and I had no control, almost passing out.

"I'm about to come..." I screamed.

Malik pumped faster until I heard him belt out a loud grunt and fall against my back.

Three hours later it was going on two a.m. and we were in the bedroom, wide awake and holding hands. His other hand was underneath the cover massaging my ass.

"What made you come over here so late?" I continued making circles on his chest. I wanted to stay like this forever, under his hold, and wake up to this familiar peace for as long as I could. Malik adjusted himself with the blanket and lifted my hand to kiss the back of my palm. I felt his heartbeat increase along with him tightening his grip around my waist as his chest rose when he began to speak.

"I went to see Alyssa a few days ago."

I tried to move out of his hold, but he wrapped his leg around my waist and turned so we could face each other.

"Before you say anything, just listen." Malik pecked my lips, and I nodded in answer.

"It better be good." I rolled my eyes.

He smirked and thrusted on top of me and I moaned, still feeling his large girth, thick and hard, pointing at my stomach since we were both naked under the covers.

"Stop playing." I pouted and pulled my lip in between my teeth.

"You're beautiful, you know that?"

"Don't try and change the subject."

"I thought I could convince her to stop fucking with my life if I could talk to her in person," Malik explained.

"Did it work?" I wrapped my arms around his neck as he buried his face in the crook of my shoulders, then trailed kisses up to my lips.

"No and Kendra was ready to fight," Malik joked and adjusted us in bed with me on top of him.

"I like Kendra."

Malik ran a hand up and down my back.

"I know and she likes you." Malik smiled at me.

"Leave Alyssa and Asia to me, that's my job."

"Yes, ma'am, and I do have another job for you," Malik said.

"Really, what is it?"

"What would you say if I told you I love you and want to be with you?" Malik questioned.

"I love you too?" I asked, shocked.

"Then I take that as a yes to being my girlfriend."

"Yeah, and you'll be my boyfriend."

"So, the first job task is taking care of this." Malik pushed upwards and I felt his erection poke me.

"What do I get if I complete my task on time?" I asked, playing along with his game.

"A raise and extra time off," Malik explained, moving his hand between us and placing his dick at my center, running it up and down my slit.

"Oka...yyy," I whispered.

"Grab the condom, baby," Malik groaned as he moved his palm up to grip my breast.

\* \* \*

A week later, I was in my office after finally getting Alyssa and Asia to come in and speak with me. They didn't know that I had either of them coming in today so this would be a big surprise, but I had plans to end this today. I called Reece over to be backup support in case I got out of character and because she had a stake in Cyrus Premier Enterprises. With Asia no longer working there they wanted to make sure to distance themselves from the drama. Malik and I made things official and we've had fun getting to know each other and spending time as a couple with our friends.

"She's here," Reece muttered, watching as Alyssa walked inside with a man I assumed was her lawyer. Malik already told me about her being pregnant and how it wasn't his since they always used protection. And they didn't have intercourse the last time they were intimate other than oral sex. My assistant pointed her toward our conference room and I smiled, then picked up my binder that held the statements they would both be making.

"They thought it would be simple and easy fucking with my clients."

"Client or boyfriend?" Reece queried.

"Both," I stated, then opened my door and walked over to my assistant's desk.

I watched from outside the clear door as Alyssa and her lawyer talked amongst themselves.

"Alyssa, and I assume you must be her lawyer, Joe Park?" I asked.

"Why are we here? I have nothing else to say about Malik and Pierce Motors," Alyssa spat. I smiled, not intimidated by her brash outburst.

"Thank you for joining me today, Alyssa. I not only work on behalf of Pierce Motors, but Cyrus Premier Enterprises which is why my colleague, Reece, is here," I replied.

"Sorry to interrupt but your other guest is here," Selena said and opened the door wider for Asia to come inside. I watched in amusement as Alyssa's mouth dropped wide open.

"What the hell is this?!" Asia snapped.

"Asia, have a seat please."

"No, because this is a setup. I don't know her." Asia pointed at Alyssa.

"Funny, because I didn't ask if you knew her. So please have a seat...now."

Asia waved me off and sat down like I said, crossing her arms and legs.

"Now that we have everyone here, I'm going to make this plain and simple."

"If you're going to try and push his agenda, it won't work. My client is innocent and only gave facts," Joe explained.

"Mr. Parks, you may want to get another client that can afford to pay you. Alyssa and Asia will be going to jail and paying back fines from all of the lies being told."

"Malik really has you delusional, girl," Asia commented.

"What's delusional is you trying to make a quick buck off a person that gave you a chance," I spat.

"Asia, why did you do this?" Reece questioned.

"Like I said, you can't prove anything," Asia replied.

"That's where you're wrong, cousin. I have photos of you and Alyssa together when you both have gone on record as not knowing each other. Also, Asia, we have computer information from you researching how to cheat in racing."

"That doesn't prove anything," Asia told me.

"Plus, the blogger has gone on record and said that you lied about everything because you wanted to get money from this deal. Only problem with that is you're going to jail," I announced.

"You're going to put your own family in jail?" Asia jumped up in shock.

"When it causes drama for my clients, I'll do anything."

"I see why Christopher dumped your ass. Stupid bitch," Asia snapped as she pushed my door open hard and stomped out of my office.

"All right, it was Asia that contacted me first," Alyssa confessed.

"Shut up, Alyssa," Joe told her.

"No, I'm not going to jail for anybody, I have a child on the way," Alyssa remarked.

"Good, so I suggest you read this statement and let everyone know you lied before these documents go to the police," I said.

"Does Malik know about this?" Alyssa questioned.

"That's none of your concern," I said.

Alyssa signed her statement in front of me and I passed it to Reece. We shook hands with her attorney as they walked out of my office. Reece and I high fived each other at sealing the deal.

# Chapter Twenty

## Sarai

Malik pulled my seat out for me at the restaurant and I sat down as he bent down to kiss me on the lips. After social media broke with Alyssa's statement and Asia finally agreeing to state on camera that she lied, we decided to come out to celebrate. It was way upscale, and I was surprised he took the day off to spend it with me. We woke up together in my bed and had breakfast then we went shopping and and watched Kamden do a few laps at Cyrus Premier Enterprises.

"Hello, I'm Deacon, your waiter for the night."

"Thanks, can we have the best champagne? We need to celebrate," Malik asked.

Deacon pulled out his iPad and put in our order of liquor and aperitifs.

"Great, I'll be back in a few minutes to take your dinner order."

"This is a nice place, Malik; I didn't think you had it in you," I giggled and he slid a hand across the table, entwining our hands.

"I am not that bad. Even if I have a reputation of not being the boyfriend type."

"You and Kamden, before he got married, were tied as the least romantic types," I joked.

"I have the Eddison blood in me, we can be romantic babies," Malik told me.

"Are you sure I'm not crashing your family barbeque?" I asked.

Malik poured our glass of wine when Deacon brought it to the table.

"No, my mom specifically wanted you to be there."

"It's weird being around them now as your girlfriend and not Arianna's friend."

Deacon placed the calamari and caviar on the table.

"Get used to it." Malik gripped my chin.

"I will."

"Are you two ready to order?" Deacon questioned and I flipped the menu back over and glanced over at the Caesar salads.

"I'll take the salad and crab cakes," I said, getting something light.

"Is that it?"

"Yep, I need to keep from eating so much. We had a big breakfast earlier, plus lunch."

"I'll take red sea pasta, steamed veggies, and steak." Malik pointed and passed his menu over.

"Awesome, you two enjoy yourselves and your food will be out soon," Deacon said, grabbing our menus.

"Tell me again how you got them to back down?" Malik inquired, taking a sip of his champagne.

"I have magic fingers."

"I can attest to your hands being magic." Malik wiggled his eyebrows at me.

I covered my mouth and giggled in embarrassment. I hadn't laughed with the opposite sex or felt comfortable with a man in a long time. He was not only sexy, funny, sweet, cocky, and on his shit as a boss. He was also a family man at heart and loved his niece and nephew.

"Do you ever want kids?" I asked curiously. At first, I never imagined wanting kids, but I believe the person you're with can help to change your mindset.

"To be honest at first, I never wanted kids. As you can see my brother and Arianna have kids and I feel like they're all I need," Malik told me.

"Same."

Ten minutes later our food came out and we talked about our plans to take a vacation together once work slowed down. He told me about a boys night coming up soon and that reminded me to have the girls over for a sleepover and night of drinking to catch up.

\* \* \*

The first touch of his tongue between my legs made me gasp. He dropped his hands to my thighs and pried them wider. I felt all logic leave my brain as our sex sessions grew even more intense as we became closer.

"Mali...kkkk." I tried to push him away as my orgasm became intense. He towered over me with his dick nudging against my pussy. I leaned up kissing down his neck right in between his Adam's apple and throat, across his six pack that led to my favorite snack.

His jaw flexed in pure pleasure.

"Please, baby..." Malik gritted through his teeth as I slid him inside me. Hearing his moans and the way I made him feel gave me pleasure. How was it possible to want to be around someone and never get tired of them? He shoved deep into me and I felt him in my stomach.

"Oh my god!"

"Fuck! Baby..." Malik lifted my legs to his shoulders.

I squeezed my eyes tight and felt the euphoria overcome me as sweat dripped down my body. Malik smacked my thigh then rubbed the sting away and I opened my eyes. He pulled out and flipped me over, with me lying flat on my stomach with his heavy body on top of mine, his warm breath next to my ear as he slipped back inside of my mound.

"I can't leave you alone," Malik moaned.

"Never leave me," I replied.

The slapping of our skin in the room grew louder as I buried my face in the covers to conceal my cries of pleasure.

"I can feel your shit choking me, baby."

"Ahhh...I'm coming again!" I screamed as I smacked the bed and tried to bite the sheets. This was the best sex of my life and I'd kill the next woman who tried to step in between us.

"Fuck! Yass..." I shouted and felt him come right behind me before he collapsed on my back. His heavy chest was almost suffocating me and peppering kisses down my back, gently moved to the side of me in the bed. I chuckled to myself that this big, tall, grumpy, and sexy man could fall to his knees when he was inside of my sex.

* * *

Two weeks later I was sitting in my office typing out a new plan for a new client I just signed to my company. Work was going well, and I decided I would try to with my mom sometime this week to see how she was doing. I had stayed away because of the mess with my cousin. I kept putting things off and she finally left me a message about having a family dinner for just the two of us.

"Hey, Sarai, you have a guest," Selena said, causing me to stop typing as I waved them inside.

"Sarai Lambert, it's nice to meet you."

"Hello, I'm sorry, who are you?"

"Sorry, I'm Detrick Reynolds." He handed me a business card and I noticed his business name was Miracle Studios. They were the biggest film studio on the East Coast and did everything from TV, film, commercials to sport events. I gestured for him to take a seat in the chair opposite my desk.

"I must say, Ms. Lambert, you're a beautiful woman," Mr. Reynolds said, licking his lips.

I ignored his flirting and cleared my throat to get the reasoning for him being here. I wouldn't say he was a bad looking guy; he was around five-eleven, lean, had a bald head and beard with full lips. Compared to Malik, I'd give him a five out of ten.

"What can I do for you, Mr. Reynolds?"

"Actually, I'm here to offer you a job," he said and pulled out a piece of paper, passing it across my desk. "As the head of Publicity for Miracle Studios, overseeing everything from film and TV, to sports, you would be the face and voice for our company."

"I'm flattered, Mr. Reynolds."

"Think about what this could mean for your name and the exposure that you'll gain beyond the racing industry," Detrick said.

"I'm pretty happy where I am now."

"You could be even happier making millions more,

think international. Make your own schedule," Detrick explained.

"How did you hear about me?" I questioned.

"It's not a secret how you were able to get Pierce Motors cleared of the cheating accusations."

"I have people in high places," I muttered, leaning back in my chair as I crossed my hands in my lap.

Having the opportunity to travel, make more money, and bring in my own clients besides who they sign?

"What about my business? I do a lot of work with Cyrus Premier Enterprises as well as charity work."

"You can continue doing that work, I would suggest you hire more staff to handle some of the workload, but don't reject the opportunity because you're scared," he said, standing up and extending his hand for a shake. "Think it over and get back to me, Sarai. This moment could be very beneficial for you."

After he left, I sat back in my seat and dialed Reece's phone number.

"Hey, Sarai," Reece said.

"I have a dilemma," I huffed as I stared at my computer screen with Malik and me from the charity race as a screensaver.

"What's up?" Reece asked. "Cyrus move."

"Cyrus's with you? Has he talked with Malik today?"

"No, should I have?" Cyrus called out.

"What's going on, Sarai? You're scaring me," Reece said.

I bit my bottom lip, twisting the phone cord in my hand.

"Don't tell Cyrus, but I got a job offer."

"Congrats! Wait, why do you sound so sad about it, girl?" Reece mumbled.

"It's with Miracle Studios in New York."

"Oh," Reece replied.

"Yep."

"Uhmm...That means you'd be moving," Reece explained.

"Yes, and I'm not sure how to handle telling Malik."

"So, you're thinking of taking the job," Reece said.

"I am and we have the family barbeque tomorrow and things are pretty serious with us now."

"I can't answer that for you, babe. You need to figure out what makes you happy, maybe long distance can work," Reece said.

"Would you do it if you were me?" I asked.

"Cyrus and I are different from you and Malik. I will say I couldn't see myself without Cyrus."

"Thanks for the advice, I'll see you at the party." I hung up the phone, continued working for the rest of the day, and went home to take a nap. I turned off my phone, wanting to be alone without the hassle of my phone going off.

# Chapter Twenty-One

## Malik

I t was the weekend and I was hanging at my parents house. Everyone was here to celebrate that we had moved on from the chaos of my love life interfering in our business. My dad was on the grill laughing with my older brother. The kids ran around the bouncy house laughing and having fun. I invited Sarai, Reece, Cyrus, and Tripp. My parents planned for a house full of people. A barbeque with friends and family and a few coworkers from Pierce Motors. Jackson was supposed to come, but JJ was sick, so he stayed home with Emery. Cyrus and Tripp walked over to me and handed me a beer.

"How are you feeling, bro?" Cyrus asked.

"I'm good, man. What's up with y'all?" I asked.

"Hungry, man. When is your pops going to stop hogging the meat?" Tripp asked, rubbing his hands together.

"You know Essence is supposed to come today."

"Is she now?" Tripp replied.

"You look like a spooked man." Cyrus clowned on him.

"Essence doesn't scare me," Tripp said, scratching the back of his head.

"Yeah right."

"Kamden just texted and said they're almost here," Cyrus stated then put his phone back in his pocket.

"He still owes me money from the last poker game," I said.

"Join the club, man. How are things with Sarai?" Cyrus asked and I glanced over at Sarai talking with my mom and Reece.

"Things are good. Almost two months of being together and things aren't hard like I thought they would be," I said as Major and Madison ran over to Sarai and pulled her arm. I lifted the beer and took a sip.

"Guess who!" Arianna covered my eyes with her hands.

"A spoiled little princess." Arianna smacked me on the back of the head.

"Ouch...Ari," I groaned, rubbing the sting out.

"Stop being an ass. I thought Sarai would have tamed you by now," Arianna remarked as she wrapped her arms around Kamden's waist.

"Did Kamden tame you?" I questioned.

"Hell no!" Kash joked.

"Kash, don't act up in front of your friends please," Arianna demanded before she rolled her eyes and tried to walk off, but he captured her hand to pull her back to his chest.

"Baby, I'm sorry," Kamden begged, sounding like a lost puppy. All three of us burst into laughter at him being weak to my sister's demands. He flipped us off and I chuckled, wondering if I acted the same way around Sarai.

"You do the same thing with Sarai," Arianna mentioned.

"No, I don't," I said.

"Do what with Sarai?" Sarai came over and stood on her tippy toes and kissed my lips.

"Nothing."

"Auntie Sarai, you got a dollar?" Major asked.

"I'm sorry, baby, I don't," Sarai said.

"What about ten dollars?" Major inquired.

Sarai looked over at me and then glanced at the rest of us and we all shrugged our shoulders. Sarai checked her pockets and pulled out some money and I held my laugh in as much as possible.

"Why do you need ten dollars, Major?" Sarai questioned.

"Because you don't have one dollar," Major said, thinking what he was saying was common knowledge.

"Do you know how I have ten dollars?" Sarai asked.

"No," Major replied.

"I work, baby, so if you want this ten dollars, I think you should do some work," Sarai said.

I was impressed she didn't let herself get played.

"I can work," Major said, jumping up and down.

"Good, so I'll give you ten dollars if you can keep an eye on your little sister for the rest of the day," Sarai remarked.

"Okay, Auntie," Major told her and ran off to Madison, little Kash, and the other kids.

"He almost played you," I said as I ran a hand up and down her back.

"I'm good at catching a game being run on me, baby."

"I see."

"Are you ready for the poker game?" Eddison Jr.

asked, and I nodded before heading toward the card table with the rest of the fellas. Thirty minutes later I was sitting across from Cyrus, Canon, Tripp, Eddison Jr., Dad, and a coworker playing poker. I was up by a hundred bucks and mostly everyone else was losing. Sarai sat on my lap as I shuffled the cards and she whispered in my ear.

"Man, do you two need to do all that lovey dovey shit all day?" Cheston, my coworker, blurted out. He was more of a friend to Canon and had nothing else to do today so I told him it was fine to come along to my parents house.

"Relax, I can't help you don't have what I got," I said and squeezed Sarai's waist and she smirked and pecked my lips.

"Most all of us got somebody right," Cyrus mentioned as Reece stood behind him.

"I should have met you first, Sarai. Malik probably doesn't know what to do with all that," Cheston joked, and I glared at him.

"I can promise Malik takes good care of me," Sarai said, turning my face to look at her and I smiled at her words. If he kept on talking shit, I can't say I'd stay off his ass if he kept bringing up Sarai's name.

"Cheston, chill out man," Canon said and passed the cigar toward him.

"I'm just having fun. Y'all too uptight," Cheston explained.

"Just focus on the game," Cyrus said.

"I like focusing on Sarai though. I heard she is getting ready to fly to the East Coast for a new job, and I'm heading that way to do some work in a few weeks," Cheston informed me and I tensed at his statement.

"Cheston, you're gonna get fucked up if you keep talking about my girl," I snapped.

"Ignore him, Malik," Sarai said.

"What? She ain't married and we know you have a roster of women lined up," Cheston said, and I wanted to ring his neck.

"Cheston, *shut up* man," Canon hissed.

"All I'm saying is that when she gets to New York I wanted to see if we could hang out," Cheston continued, and I jumped up. Cyrus, Canon, and Eddison, Jr. tried to hold me back.

"Get the fuck out of here before I kick your ass!" I shouted.

"Malik! Calm down, he's not worth it," Sarai said, rubbing my back to calm me.

Cheston laughed at my outburst and I could tell he was a little drunk.

"Malik, you ain't always going to be around. I mean it didn't last long with her ex, so you might as well cut your losses," Cheston said.

"Motherfuc—"

"Malik!" Sarai screamed when I pushed all of them away and punched Cheston in the face. I didn't stop until I heard the kids crying and screaming my name.

"What the hell is wrong with you!" Sarai shouted.

"Nothing besides I refuse to let another man disrespect my girl."

"Men hit on me all day, Malik, get over it and act like you have some sense," Sarai stated and tried to walk off.

"Where are you going?" I questioned.

"Home. I need to think," Sarai said.

"I'll come with you," I said.

"No, you need to stay and help your family clean up," Sarai said.

I watched my brother and Canon lift Cheston and take him into the house. Sarai walked off with Reece, mumbling about me acting a damn fool.

"Give her some time." Cyrus came over with a towel filled with ice to wrap around my hand.

"This love shit is driving me crazy," I said.

"Did she tell you about her moving away?" Cyrus announced.

"Wait... what?"

"I thought she would have spoken to you earlier or maybe Reece," Cyrus said.

"So, what Cheston said is true?" I questioned.

"I got her letter of resignation a few days ago. Said she was quitting and moving to New York."

"That's some bullshit!" I yelled and tried to run into the house. Cyrus and Kamden stepped in front of me to hold me back. "When was she going to tell me?" I asked out loud.

"Malik, you need to get control of yourself and tell me why I have someone in my bathroom bleeding half to death," Mom said.

"Ma, not right now."

"He's pissed about Sarai," Eddison Jr. told her.

"What about her?" Mom asked.

"She got a job offer," Eddison Jr. said.

"That's a good thing, right?" Mom stated.

"In New York and she hadn't said one thing to me, her boyfriend," I spat, leaving the backyard and heading inside. I found Sarai and Reece talking with Canon as Cheston held an ice pack against his face. I reached out

167

and pulled Sarai aside so we could to talk alone and she jerked out of my hold.

"I need to talk to you," I said.

"When you calm down, we can talk," Sarai stated.

"Are you moving to New York?" I blurted out.

Sarai sighed, rubbing her hands up and down her arms. "I haven't made up my mind yet. I was waiting to talk to you about everything." I crossed my arms over my chest and waited to see if she was serious.

"When was that going to happen?" I questioned.

"Malik, it's not like I'm moving tomorrow, and the opportunity just came to me a few weeks ago," Sarai stated.

"So, you've known this information for weeks and didn't tell me?"

"You're taking it out of context," Sarai mentioned, and I waved her off.

"No, I thought my girlfriend would have enough sense that she would talk with me as soon as she was approached about something that could change our lives."

"You know what? I'm not talking about this right now," Sarai told me and turned back to Reece.

"You're right, we don't have to talk about this right now or ever. Have fun in New York at your new job," I said and walked off.

"Malik, what does that mean?" Sarai asked, jumping in front me to stop me from leaving.

"Means congrats! Don't worry about discussing anything with me. Live your life without thinking of the people that should be included in decisions," I argued and grabbed my jacket to leave.

I jumped in my car and drove off as Sarai, Reece, and my family came outside, blowing up my phone. I wasn't planning on going to my condo since they'd check there first, so I turned into traffic, picking up speed. A car horn honked when I cut them off and I flipped them off, hopping on the freeway.

Thoughts of Sarai leaving me after I confessed to loving her when I'd never been in love with someone before swirled in my head. Sarai thought I was only mad that she got an opportunity in New York, but it was deeper than that because she never included me in her decisions. Maybe I should have kept things simple with us from the beginning; just sexual and nothing more, because it'd take me time to get over her.

"Fuck!" I slapped my hand against the steering wheel.

I turned into the driveway of my beach house and cut off my car, jumped out, and felt my phone vibrating in my pocket. I'd never been the jealous type and something came over me when Cheston kept taunting me about Sarai and how she would be out in New York, alone and free to do whatever with whoever.

I pushed my key into the door and kicked off my shoes, removing my shirt, and walked into the bathroom to wash my hands again. I looked in the mirror and saw stress already showing on my face. I sighed and picked up the towel and grabbed the alcohol, Neosporin, and gauze to clean my hand. I heard my phone ringing, and I lifted it up and saw my mom calling.

"Yeah," I answered, sitting down on the couch.

"Thank God you're safe," Mom said.

"Sorry about running out, Ma, but I needed a minute."

"I understand, Malik, but when you're in a relationship you don't run out on your significant other because you're upset," Mom chastised me.

"I hear you and I won't have to worry about that next time, because I'm done with relationships."

"You don't mean that."

"I do, so tell everybody not to worry. If Sarai asks you anything, tell her have fun," I said and hung up the phone, tossed it on the couch, then leaned my head back on the couch and closed my eyes.

*Buzz buzz!*

I groaned and picked up my phone again.

*Baby: You're really breaking up with me?*

*Me: I don't do liars.*

*Baby: I didn't lie, I was going to talk to you.*

*Me: Yeah almost a month late.*

*Baby: Malik get over yourself.*

*Me: Yeah and you do the same.*

I closed out of the phone and stretched out on the couch to sleep for the rest of the day.

# Chapter Twenty-Two

## Sarai

A month later I was in New York on a tour at Miracle Studios, meeting all of the staff and crew I would be working with on my campaigns. After the big blowup happened with Malik, I stopped trying to get him to listen to me and I wouldn't apologize when I didn't feel like I did anything wrong. Yes, I should have consulted him a little earlier. But I needed a moment to really take in the opportunity that was being presented as a career move.

My mom was at my place, helping me unpack, and I would be meeting her for lunch soon. Detrick was cool and not as much of a jerk as I thought he would be and he helped me find a place to stay near Manhattan. I hoped to purchase a house outside of the city soon and have my mom move here for good. Even though our relationship took a few hits we'd gotten better with our communication.

"This is Robert, the account manager," Detrick said, knocking on the door of Robert's office. I reached a hand out to shake and he grasped my palm and greeted me.

"Nice to meet you, Sarai," Robert said.

"Thank you."

"Do you need anything else? I have another meeting that I have to attend," Detrick spoke.

"No, I have a lunch meeting and then need to unpack before I start holding meetings," I said.

"Great. Let me know if you need me for anything else, you can call me at any time," Detrick stated and escorted me back to my office. I waved goodbye, picked up my cell phone, and noticed a call from Reece. I dialed her number and she picked up on the first ring.

"Hey, New Yorker," Reece teased.

"Hey, Reece, when are you guys coming up here?" I asked.

"I don't know, I have too much work to do and Cyrus is slammed with his races," Reece explained.

"How is Arianna doing?" I asked.

"She's good, running behind Kamden and little Kash as usual."

"What about Cyrus?"

"Just ask, Sarai, and stop going around the subject," Reece told me.

"I don't know what you're talking about."

"You don't want to know about Malik?" Reece challenged.

I picked up my cup of coffee and took a sip while opening my welcome email from Miracle Studios.

"No."

"I'm starting to think you two are acting childish," Reece said.

"I have too much going on to focus on the past. Besides, men come and go, I'll have another one soon."

"He won't be Malik though," Reece stated.

"Whose side are you on?"

"Sarai, you know I'm always on your side, same as Arianna when she had her blowup with Kash," Reece explained.

"And?"

"And you both need to understand that it takes two people to make a relationship work," Reece stated.

"You think I gave up too easily?"

"He's not Christopher and you gave him multiple chances," Reece insisted.

"Someone woke up on the shady side today," I chuckled, closed out my computer and grabbed my laptop computer, sliding it in my carrying case.

"Shade you out of love, but seriously I'm proud of you and want you to be happy no matter who you're with," Reece said.

I turned the chair around and pushed it up against the desk, then checked the time on my watch.

"Thanks, boo. Let me get out of here and head home. My mom is still unpacking for me."

"Call me later after you're settled," Reece said, and I agreed, hanging up the phone and turning the light off in the office. I closed my office door and waved goodbye to my assistant. Miracle Studios occupied over three thousand square feet of office with offsite shooting space for tv and film sets.

I hopped in my car and drove back to my condo, which was twenty minutes from the studios, and hit the bluetooth on my car to dial my assistant back in California. I was lucky to still be able to run my business even though I stepped down from Cyrus Premier Enterprises and Pierce Motors. I couldn't give up on my regular clients who were with me in the beginning, so I had Sarah oversee everything by hiring her as a full-time publicist and got an assistant to help her out. She was capable of running the office on her own, but I still checked in when I could.

"Hey, Sarai," Sarah spoke when the call connected.

"What's going on, Sarah?" I asked as I turned into traffic.

"Nothing much, it's quiet over here," Sarah said.

"That's a good thing. I saw the photos from the premier of Jasmine's movie. Great job and interview," I told her.

"I learned from you."

I pulled up to the four-way stop and waited a second before pulling into my residential area. I parked in front of my building and turned the car off.

"You did it on your own and I can see you opening your own place soon," I remarked.

"I'm good working for Lambert Publicity," Sarah said.

We ended the call, and I got out of the car and walked up to my door, unlocking it and going inside, then off turned the alarm.

"Mom, I'm home!" I yelled and picked up my mail and walked through my living room with all the boxes sitting around.

"You're home," Mom said. I walked up and kissed her cheek before plopping down on the couch, kicking my feet up.

"How was your first day?" Mom questioned.

"It was fine, mostly meeting the bigwigs and my staff."

"You're in charge of a team of people?"

"Yep, a whole department wing is dedicated to marketing, your daughter is a very important person at the company."

"I'm proud of you, Sarai. I know I was wrong for sticking up for Asia, but I felt bad for her never getting ahead of things," Mom explained. I removed my heels and dropped my mail on the table and took off my jacket.

"Has she tried to call you at all?"

Mom nodded in answer and I scoffed that Asia thought she could get in good with my mom to ask me for money. Last I heard she was living in a small apartment with some guy who wasn't good for her at all. He mostly cheated on her and barely paid any of the bills.

"Yes, and no I didn't give her any money," Mom said.

"Good."

"What about you and your love life?" Mom asked.

"I have no love life. Well, work is my love life right now."

"He hasn't called you at all?"

"If he has, I don't know because I blocked his number," I said, then stood up to go into my bedroom to change into something more comfortable.

"Can you order a pizza? I'm going to change and finish unpacking."

"Sure baby," Mom said, grabbing the phone as I walked to the bedroom and listened to her and stepped out of my skirt. I opened the dresser drawer and pulled out a pair of shorts and a t-shirt to change into. I strolled out of the bedroom and grabbed a box of books and moved it to the floor in front of my bookcase. I started pulling out my books and placing them in order of genre and with my favorite authors up top. The doorbell rang and my mom picked the money off the table to pay for the pizza and tip the driver.

"Look what I found," Mom said, and I looked behind

me to see Reece, Arianna, and Essence holding bottles of wine and pizza.

"Oh my god! What are you doing here?" I shouted and jumped up, running toward them.

"Surprise!" Essence screamed.

"I see that," I said dryly.

"We wanted to come surprise you since I have a photo shoot out here in few days," Arianna mentioned.

"Did Kamden come with you?" I inquired, feeling like they were keeping something from me.

"He's back home with little Kash," Arianna replied.

"I'm happy you guys came! It feels like old times."

# Chapter Twenty-Three

## Malik

I slammed the phone down and shoved everything off my desk. For the past two weeks, I'd done nothing but work and try to get in touch with Sarai, but she'd been avoiding my calls. When I first ended things, I was high on my emotions and not thinking straight. I let Cheston get in my head. Canon told me he never went to New York, so I was worried about nothing.

"Fuck!" I shouted.

Kendra ran inside. "What's wrong?"

"Nothing."

"I hope you know I'm not cleaning this mess up."

"Kendra not now," I muttered.

"Then when, Malik? You've done nothing but mope around here for the past few weeks."

I grunted and sat forward in my seat, thinking over my next step.

"I don't mope," I said.

"You're right. It's not moping, I call it being an ass," Kendra insisted and came forward to take a seat.

"You think I was wrong?"

"Most definitely."

"I can't lose her Kendra."

"I don't know what to tell you, Malik. You used to let people explain themselves," Kendra explained.

"She took another job without talking to me about how it would make me feel."

"Malik, you sound like the typical male that wants everything handed to you," Kendra spat and stood up.

"I take responsibility for my part, but she's not innocent," I replied.

"Listen, she received an opportunity to better things for her career. I would do the same. It's about how you support her if you truly love her."

"I hear you, Kendra."

"You hear me, but are you *listening*?" Kendra questioned, shaking her head and walking out of my office. I scanned the mess I made and yelled for her to get the cleaning staff.

"Nope, clean it up yourself!" Kendra shouted.

* * *

Once work was done for the day and I hung with my father for lunch, I invited him and the rest of the guys over for poker night. Cicely hooked us up with everything from sub sandwiches and burgers, to hotdogs, potato salads, and veggie trays with different dressings.

Canon popped the bottle of scotch open.

"Let me get a glass of that," Kash said as he passed his glass over.

"Do we have any vodka?" I called out as he stood at the bar preparing his drink.

"Yeah. Here you go," Canon stated.

"Who wants a cigar?" Dad asked.

"Me," Cyrus, Canon, and I said at the same time.

"Cuban cigars are the best," Canon stated, walking back over to his chair.

"Have you talked to Arianna yet?" I questioned Kamden and everyone got quiet.

"What?"

"She's good," Kamden said.

"The shoot is tomorrow, right?" I investigated.

"Uhmm... yeah," Kash said.

I chuckled at his weirdness. "What's wrong with you?"

"She's with Sarai and Reece," Cyrus blurted out.

"That's cool, I figured they would see each other when she visited."

"You're not upset?" Canon wondered.

"At this point she's made it clear we both have to move on."

"I feel you went overboard, but that's just me," Canon said as he shuffled the cards.

"Cyrus, tell me how many times you've had to almost wring some guy's neck that overstepped?"

"One time we were in the club, and Reece was trying to make me jealous, and I almost kicked a guy's ass that tried to act bold," Cyrus explained.

"I remember Arianna trying to make me jealous in a club too. What's wrong with those girls?" Kamden said.

"It's called not having trust in your partner," Dad said.

"Pops you've been married forever," I said.

"Which means you should take my advice."

"I've been married to your sister for a year, and it's not

all peaches and cream. Your dad's right about trust in a relationship," Kamden told me.

"Communication and trust will carry you a long way in a relationship," Dad said.

I nodded my head and thought back to one of our many dates and the way I was changing around her.

*Flashback*

*I laid the paper plates down on the blanket and picked up our napkins and food from the shack, which I unwrapped. She smiled, grabbed the plate out of my hand, and sat with her legs crossed in front of her.*

*"I love these sandwiches," Sarai said, taking a bite and wiping her mouth with the napkin.*

*"Cyrus introduced me to them, and I've been addicted ever since."*

*"I'm surprised you would do something like this honestly."*

*"What, the romantic type?" I asked.*

*She nodded and took a sip of the apple cider champagne.*

*"Yep, I thought you'd be the Netflix and chill type," Sarai teased.*

*"See, that's what you get for assuming. But I do have my moments when the right person comes along."*

*"So, I'm the right person?" Her right eyebrow lifted in question.*

*"I admit, I've never done this with a woman outside a hotel stay."*

*"Ooh. You're the bring them to a hotel so they don't know where you lay your head type." Sarai giggled.*

*I was amazed at the beautiful smile on her face and I pushed a piece of curly hair behind her ear. I took a bite of my sandwich and continued watching the sunset.*

*"This is beautiful."*

*"It is," I replied, staring at her.*

*"Tell me, Malik, what are your intentions?" Sarai asked.*

*"My intentions are to make you my girlfriend."*

*"Mmmmm...I've had a bad relationship before. I can't go down that road again."*

*"We can make it work if we trust each other."*

*"Have you ever had a relationship?" she questioned.*

*I wiped the little piece of sauce on her bottom lip with my thumb and kissed her lips.*

*"No, but I won't lie to you and say I'm perfect."*

*"So, I'm practice for you?"*

*I chuckled, placed my sandwich down along with hers, and pulled her on top of my chest, caressing up and down her back.*

*"You're Sarai and I'm Malik, two people that like each other and want to continue getting to know each other."*

*I leaned up and pecked her lips twice.*

*"Plus, you have me addicted to what's between your legs now and I can't let anyone else have a taste," I joked.*

*Sarai rolled her eyes and we stayed outside watching the waves until the weather turned colder.*

Present Day

"Yo, Malik, where did you go?" Canon asked as he waved his hand in front of my face.

"Uhm...Cyrus I need to grab a ride."

"To where? Your car's outside," Cyrus replied, laughing.

"I mean a ride on your jet. I'm going to New York," I said. The guys clapped in excitement and my dad reached over, grinned, and patted me on the back.

"Good job, son," Dad said.

# Chapter Twenty-Four

## Sarai & Malik

**S***arai*

*Bang! Bang!*

I checked the clock and it said six a.m. I was still hungover from another night of us partying and drinking together. The girls were sleeping and I'd planned for us to go shopping today since it was the weekend and I didn't need to be at work until Monday. At one point, someone decided bang on my door so my mom talked me into getting a bat and taser for protection since I'd be living alone. The banging continued, and I tossed the covers back and jumped up, grabbed my robe and the bat next to my bed, and walked out of my room as Arianna snored in my bed. Reece and Essence slept in the guestroom while my mom stayed out on the couch. *Nobody else hears this?* I yanked the door open before I checked who was on the other side and gasped in shock.

"Malik?"

"Sarai."

"Do you know what time it is?" I asked and closed my robe.

"Sorry, I needed to see you."

"At six in the morning? Did someone die?" I snapped.

He tried to move forward but I held my hand up to block him.

"Can we talk?" Malik questioned.

"Fine," I said and stood to the side, letting him in. Malik looked around my living room and waited for me to say something. My mother stirred from her sleep getting up to leave, taking the blanket and pillows and went to the bedroom, and waved at him.

"Come inside," I said as I strolled to the kitchen and grabbed a bottle of water.

"Thanks," Malik said.

"All right, so what's so important you needed to see me at six in the morning?"

"I want to apologize to you for not listening and communicating and letting things go on this long."

"I appreciate your apology."

"I fucked up, Sarai, and I want a second chance to get it right."

"You royally fucked up."

"Is it too late?" Malik inquired as he lifted my hand and caressed my palm.

"Why should I, Malik? You acted like an ass at the party and then you wouldn't take my calls."

"You're right, but I don't want this to end."

"It ended when you blew up at me."

"I can admit my wrongs and the way I handled that situation was stupid. You're the best thing that's ever happened to me."

"What's all the noise?" Arianna asked as she walked into the living room.

"Sorry, Princess," Malik stated.

"Malik! What are you doing here?" Arianna asked.

"I needed to see Sarai," Malik said and lifted me ontothe couch.

"What are you doing?" I asked.

"Sarai, why are you? Malik, you're here," Reece exclaimed and hugged Arianna in surprise.

"Reece, you knew about this, didn't you?" I asked, annoyed.

"No, Cyrus just texted me though," Reece said and flipped her phone around to show us.

"Sarai, will you please give me a second chance and be my girlfriend?" Malik asked.

"I don't do the whole 'shutting me out because you're pissed off and not taking my calls' thing, Malik."

"I know and I promise moving forward we'll talk about everything as a couple," Malik spoke, resting his hand on my thigh.

"I apologize for blocking your number."

He emphasized, cupped my chin. "We both acted poorly. I apologize on my end."

"What about my job? I'm not leaving, so if you're going to ask me to quit that's not happening," I said.

"I know and I wouldn't ask you to do anything like that," Malik said.

"So will it be long distance then?"

"I'm the soon-to-be CEO of Pierce Motors, we have an office here in New York I can work out of. I'll follow you where you allow me to go," he said and wrapped his arms around my waist.

"I'm so glad you two are going to try again," Reece said.

"Seriously because Sarai is grouchy without you, bro," Arianna mentioned. Malik leaned down, capturing my lips, and I moaned into his kiss and pulled back when I realized I hadn't brushed my teeth.

* * *

## Malik

"I need to brush my teeth," Sarai said.

"I don't care, I just miss being in your presence."

Sarai wrapped her arms around my neck and stood on her tippy toes to kiss me deeply.

"So, you're going to move here for real?" Sarai asked.

"Yes, and I want to apologize, because I was holding some resentments from my issues with Alyssa and women I've dealt with in the past and held them over your head."

"Sarai, do you know what time it is?" DeeDee asked as she strolled back up front.

"Sorry, we have a visitor," Sarai replied and stepped out of my hold.

"I see," DeeDee said.

"Hi, Ms. DeeDee," I said.

"You get your mind together, Malik?" DeeDee questioned.

"Yes, and I won't be stepping out of line again."

"Good, because Sarai has gone through a lot of pain in the past," DeeDee explained.

"Ma, don't start please," Sarai said.

"I won't say another word. Just be careful with her heart," DeeDee stated.

"I need a shower," Sarai said and walked toward her bedroom.

"What are your plans for today?" I asked, following her to the back. Arianna was packing her things in her luggage.

"What are you doing, Arianna?" Sarai questioned, looking through her closet for something to wear.

"Kamden texted and said he's on his way to pick me up. We're going to stay at a hotel."

"Y'all can stay here," Sarai mentioned.

"I think you and Malik need a little alone time," Arianna teased.

"Are Reece and Essence going too?" Sarai asked.

"Yep, Cyrus is with him," Arianna said just as the doorbell rang. I walked back into the living room and opened the door, slapped hands with them both as Reece and Essence came out rolling their luggage.

Reece and Essence passed their bags to Cyrus, and DeeDee came out a few minutes later with her luggage.

"I already told her I was leaving to give you two alone time. I like you, Malik, and want some grandbabies one day," DeeDee said.

"Are you flying back with Reece and Cyrus?" I questioned.

"Yes, and if I hear you acting a fool out here, I'll hop back on a plane," DeeDee challenged, pointing her finger at me.

"Yes ma'am." I laughed and kissed her on the cheek.

A few minutes later, Arianna came out dressed in jeans and a shirt, lifting her bag over her shoulder.

"I'll take that, baby," Kash said.

"Talk to you guys later," I said and shut the door when I heard the shower turn on in the bathroom. I removed my jacket and kicked off my shoes and walked into her bathroom staring at her silhouette in the shower.

"Are you going to join me?" Sarai asked.

"I can't promise to take it easy," I said before I lifted my white t-shirt off and removed my pants and boxers. I slid the shower door open and stepped up against her back and wrapped my arms around her waist, kissing the back of her neck. A wave of primal heat surged over me as my palm ran across her stomach, up her chest, and gripped her left breast. Moving my hand down, I inserted an index finger in her sex. I felt her shiver in anticipation at my dick entering her from the back as she lifted up on her toes and arched her back as we both moaned in satisfaction.

"Ohhh..."

"Shit! This feels like I never left," I said.

"Ughhh... shit," Sarai cried out.

"Spread your legs a little more, baby."

The water trickled down our bodies as her head laid against the wall.

"Aghhhh... God damn... I'm sorry I hurt you," I groaned, fondling her breast. I pulled out and stroked my dick, trying to avoid coming too early. Sarai turned around and I lifted her. She grasped my dick and lined it up with her center and eased down as I buried my head in her neck to avoid crying out. Our kiss grew hotter, deeper, more intense as my strokes went faster and I spread her legs wider, gripping her ass cheeks tighter.

"Ahhh ..." Sarai whimpered, biting down on my neck.

"Come for me, baby," I said.

"Oh God! Yesss...right there," Sarai screamed as I rocked back and forth and growled in her ear. Her breathing escaped soft in and out. I lowered her down and grabbed the soap and towel to wash her off. She did the same for me as we continued kissing. Ten minutes later we stepped out of the shower and ordered food to be delivered and decided to kick it together and continue talking and figuring out our next steps.

# Chapter Twenty-Five

## Malik

One week later
"Ladies and gentlemen, please stand for the national anthem," the announcer stated. Sarai flew back to California with me for the race we had scheduled that Cyrus was driving in against our team. I was standing next to the pit watching as Kamden and Cyrus were giving interviews and our friends and family stood in the stands. Reece walked over to me.

"How are you feeling?" Reece asked.

"I'm good. Did you get it?" I questioned.

She opened the bag and I picked up the small black box and opened it. A ten-carat diamond shaped in the form of a heart with our initials engraved on it sat inside.

"She's going to be so surprised," Reece said.

The cars lined up, ready to go, as the clock counted down. I heard screams for Cyrus and Kash from fans as cameras continued to take shots of them.

"I hope she says yes."

"I can't imagine her saying anything but yes. You've

both come together, learned what works for you in a relationship," Reece said. "And she loves you, Malik."

"Yeah, I know because she cursed my ass out when I flew to New York," I joked.

"I'm happy for you two and believe me, it wasn't always perfect between me and Cyrus," Reece explained.

"He told me how you guys went back and forth for a while before you got it together."

"Yep, and did he tell you I couldn't stand him at first? He was making out with another person at the auction," Reece stated.

"I remember him telling us how you were stuck in a closet together."

"Not the most romantic situation to talk about to friends and family."

"Thanks for not turning your back on me. I know you're best friends with Sarai and you have no loyalty to me."

"I'm here for you both, Malik. I want you both to be happy," Reece said and locked her arm in mine as we walked over to the stands as the race was ending.

"Hey, are we going to dinner?" Sarai asked.

I slipped the box in my pocket, checked my watch. I had dinner planned for the entire family at the restaurant and I was planning on proposing, but as I looked at her now, I couldn't wait any longer. I dropped to my knee and the entire crowd started to shout and cheer. Sarai looked shocked and surprised. I wore jeans with a suit jacket today to be a little more comfortable.

I grabbed her hand and kissed the back of her palm. Sarai's hand flew to her mouth.

"Malik, what are you doing?"

"Sarai, I know I don't deserve you. I've had more than

enough time to know that any man on this earth would be breaking down your door."

"Yeah, Uncle Malik!" Madison screamed.

I chuckled at her enthusiasm.

"The second you walked into my office, I said to myself that you would bring me to my knees. Even when I messed us up and we broke up I knew you were the one for me," I stated.

A tear slid down her cheek.

"Baby, I love you and I will do everything in my power to love you the way you deserve to be loved. Will you marry me?" I asked.

Sarai looked over at her mom and aunt. Then my parents and Reece.

"Yes! I'll marry you, Malik," Sarai said as I slid the ring on her finger and stood up to kiss her on the lips, pulling her into my chest. The entire crowd stood up and clapped in joy as engines roared and Cyrus did a lap around the track for us. I pecked her lips one more time and pulled back.

"I love you," Sarai said.

"I love you, baby."

# Epilogue: Malik

Three months later

I heard a knock on the door so I walked out of the kitchen and answered it, staring at my sister and her husband kissing with little Kash standing next to them covering his face in embarrassment. I bent down to pick him up and kissed his cheek.

"Little man, I feel the same way," I said, stepping to the side to let them in. Ari and Kamden pulled back from each other and walked inside.

"Hey, Malik," Ari said, hugging me around the waist.

"What's up, little girl?" I asked, hugging her back.

She hit me on my shoulder and walked past with her hand rubbing against her stomach that held my future nephew. When they found out she was pregnant with another boy, she was pissed at first, but she got over it after a while. Kash followed behind, extending his hand for me to shake. I sat little Kash down on the floor and he took off running and fell flat on his face trying to catch up with his mom.

"What smells good?" Kamden asked.

191

"Sarai cooked baked chicken, shrimp, lobster, fresh pasta, and vegetables," I replied.

Kamden nodded and picked up little Kash to wipe his face.

"He's just like his mommy and you fall for it," I joked.

"Don't remind me, she's so damn spoiled," Kamden replied and stepped into the dining room of my house. Our whole family and our friends came over to have lunch with us. Sarai couldn't wait to announce our good news and I told her bringing everyone together would be better than calling folks individually. Cicely came over earlier to help cook and set things up, even Jackson and Emery came with the kids. I watched as my family laughed and talked together. Even loudmouth Essence came to have lunch since she was supposed to hang with Ari. Sarai hugged her mom and passed the pitcher of sangria around the table. She wasn't drinking but everyone else could indulge. I had my bottle of beer ready to gulp down. Sarai looked over at me and smiled. She waved for me to come toward her and I kissed her cheek when I got beside her.

"How are the wedding plans going?" Reece asked.

"We haven't even started yet. Our work is taking up so much time," Sarai said.

"Hell, I'll take her to the courthouse if she wants to, but I'm patient."

"Uncle Malik, you have a dollar?" Madison stood up in her chair and asked.

"Madison, I thought we talked about this," I said.

"You talked, I didn't listen though," Madison replied and everyone laughed.

I pulled out my wallet and handed her a dollar.

"I wanted to get you a wedding gift," Madison said.

"That's sweet, princess, how much do you have saved up?" I asked.

She tapped her chin in thought.

"I have two hundred dollars saved up," Madison said excitedly.

"Well in that case, can I have a dollar?" I asked.

"No, sorry I'm broke," Madison said, and we burst out in laughter at her comment.

The rest of the afternoon we laughed, talked, and hung out with our family and friends. This was the future I was meant to have. Sarai Lambert was the definition of the type of pressure that I wanted to keep me on my toes because the smile on her face made me whole.

* * *

I hope you enjoyed Sarai and Malik's story. Check the sneak peek of "**Ride: Pierce Motors Book 3**" on the next page. If you love romantic comedy, fake relationships, enemies to lovers, find it here in "**Something Gained.**" Click the link here https://books2read.com/u/baGLYy. My stories of friends finding love started with the Heart of Stone series that includes a host of characters and family. "**Broken**" Follow Emery and Jackson in a sports, one night stand, workplace romance: https://books2read.com/u/3LoelX

Then you can continue with a fun side story of Emery and Jackson with "Valentine's Day" short here: https://books2read.com/u/4jAypY

Jordan's story continues in "**Rebirth**" book 2, a single dad, widow billionaire romance found here: https://books2read.com/u/ba2OMx

\* \* \*

Please also check out a second-chance workplace romance here, "**Renew Book 4**" https://books2read.com/u/4NXyPG with a host of characters intertwined.

Follow Desiree and Gabriel in "**Temptation**" a standalone contemporary, sports, curvy girl romance. Check it out here https://books2read.com/u/mle1Vv

Check out dark mafia romance here that started my journey with Antonio and Sabrina in "**Ruthless Book 1**" https://books2read.com/u/4AxKLo

The relationship continues in "**Savage**" book 2 as they get to know each other and their families: https://books2read.com/u/bpED6g

Antonio and Sabrina have more work to do in "**Beast**" book 3 right here: https://books2read.com/links/ubl/4AxKOd

\* \* \*

Did you know Janice and Carlo have a book? Well grab this dark mafia romance with emotional scars, and betrayal right here: https://books2read.com/u/b6je6M

Any fans of forbidden romance, political? Check out "**Mutual Agreement**" https://books2read.com/u/mgzzWX a steamy romance. Pre-order the full novel of "**Nasir**" click the link here.

Have you checked out "**She's All I Need**" click here https://books2read.com/u/49lkeW a sports, opposites attract romance. What about dark romance that has everything from steamy romance, opposites attract, suspense, thriller, celebrity, and more "**Stolen Book 1**" https://books2read.com/u/mvZlgV Don't miss the follow up Joaquin and Sofia's story in book 2 "**Saved**" https://books2read.com/u/4DWwLd

The conclusion for Joaquin and Sofia comes full circle in "**Betrayed**" here: https://books2read.com/u/4A5LGp

\* \* \*

Catch up with favorite characters in this holiday short romance which includes spoilers. "**Holiday collection**" here https://books2read.com/u/bzd59G

For small town, single mom stories check out "**Until Seren**a" https://books2read.com/u/mej8vr. All curvy girl, plus size romance lovers get into "**I Deserve His Love**" a standalone, second chance romance here: https://books2read.com/u/mVrGwP

The fantasy romance readers look no further than a "**Red Light District**" a curvy girl, fling romance here: https://books2read.com/u/m2RQ6G

# Sneak Peek: Ride

***Can this bad boy race car driver navigate his way to love?***

Amena had her dream job as stylist to the rich and famous, but her dreams were cut short when her boyfriend put her through a terrible break up, leaving her to raise their child alone. Now she only has one focus, being the best single mom she can be and getting her life back on track.

Laikin's lived for the thrill of the race. As a hotshot driver, fame and groupies have become part of his life. Trying to escape the city he takes a peaceful drive, not expecting to find a damsel in distress on the side of the road.

Both Laikin and Amena are taken on a trip down memory lane when he stops to help her. She's the woman that broke his heart, and he's the crush she allowed to slip away. They're not the same people the used to be, but their feelings for each other haven't changed at all.

***Can Laikin convince Amena to give him a***

*second chance, or is his fame and the constant throng of groupies going to force her to turn away before they reach the finish line?*

# WHAT'S NEXT?!

Want to know what happens next?

Follow me on social media to catch the next release.

Reviews are the lifeblood of the publishing world. They're read, appreciated, and needed. Please consider taking the time to leave a few words on Goodreads, or bookbub.

Sign up for updates and sneak peaks at the site below.

https://www.bookbub.com/chiquitadennie

https://www.chiquitadennie.com

https://www.goodreads.com/author/chiquitadennie

https://Facebook.com/chiquitassteamyreadinggroup

x.com/authorchiquitad

https://www.instagram.com/authorchiquitadennie

https://www.Facebook.com/authorchiquitadennie

https://www.304publishing.tumblr.com

Thank you so much for reading and if you enjoyed the crazy ride and decide to leave a review we truly appreciate the support.

# About the Author

Chiquita Dennie is an author of Contemporary, Romantic Suspense, Erotic, and Women's Fiction.

Chiquita lives in Los Angeles, CA. Before she started writing contemporary romance, she worked in the entertainment industry on notable TV shows such as the Dr. Phil show, the Tyra Banks show, American Idol, and Deal or No Deal. But her favorite job is the one she's now doing: full-time writing romance.

A best-selling author and award-winning filmmaker, her first short film, "Invisible," was released in summer 2017 and screened in multiple festivals and won for Best Short Film. She also hosts a podcast that showcases the latest in beauty, business, and community called "Moscato and Tea." Her debut release of *Antonio and Sabrina Struck in Love* has opened a new avenue of writing that she loves. Nominated for 2021 Author of the Year, Best Black Romance "Mutual Agreement," and Best Interracial Romance for "She's All In Need". In 2022 nominated Author Queen of the Year, Best Black Romance "Nasir" Best Interracial Romance "Torn" and Best Romantic Comedy "Something Gained" by Black Girls Who Write.

If you want to know when the next book will come out, please visit my website at http://www.chiquitaden nie.com, where you can sign up to receive an email for my next release.

# Acknowledgments

A huge thank you to my team that helps me behind the scenes, from my editors, test readers, graphic designers, and the list goes on. Truly appreciate each of you for keeping me on my toes.

# Pressure Playlist
## @304publishing

1. Beyonce: Blow
2. Rihanna: Sex with Me
3. Tank: When We Make Love
4. Monica: Superman
5. Mario: Let Me Love You
6. Justin Timberlake: Mirror
7. Megan The Stallion: Don't Stop
8. Avant: Read Your Mind
9. SWV: Weak
10. Marvin Gaye: Let's Get On

# Also by Chiquita Dennie

**Series**

**Struck in Love**

The Early Years-A Prequel Short Story

Ruthless:Antonio and Sabrina Book 1

Savage: Antonio and Sabrina Book 2

Beastl: Antonio and Sabrina Book 3

Captivated By His Love:Janice and Carlo

Brutal: Antonio and Sabrina Booke 4

Redemption: Antonio and Sabrina Book 5

**Heart of Stone**

Broken, Book 1 (Emery & Jackson)

A Valentine's Day Short Book 1.5 Emery & Jackson

Rebirth, Book 2 (Jordan and Damon)

Reveal, Book 3 (Angela and Brent)

Bottoms Up Book 3.5 Jessica and Joseph Short

Renew, Book 4 (Jessica and Joseph)

**Cocky Billionaire Boys**

Cocky Catcher (Cocky Billionaire Boys Book 1)

Bossy Billionaire (Cocky Billionaire Boys Book 2)

**The Fuertes Cartel**

Stolen (The Fuertes Cartel Book 1)

Saved (The Fuertes Cartel Book 2)

Betrayed (The Fuertes Cartel Book 3)

## **Carrington Cartel**

Torn: The Carrington Cartel Book 1

Claim: The Carrington Cartel Book 2

## **Something**

Something Gained: A Romantic Comedy Book 1

Something Earned: A Romantic Comedy Book 2

## **Pierce Motors**

Refuel:( Pierce Motors Book l)

Pressure:( Pierce Motors Book 2)

## **Summer Break**

Summer Nights( Summer Break Book 1)

## **TN Seal Security**

Aydin: Book 1

Nasir: Book 2

Nicco: Book 3

## **Standalones**

Until Serena(HEA World Novel)

Temptation

She's All I Need

I Deserve His Love

Mutual Agreement

Scoring with Sadie

Exposed (A Bodyguard Novel)

Love Shorts:A Collection of Short Stories

Red Light District(A Fantasy Romance Short)

## By Keke Renée:

Wet Heat

His Peace, Her Pleasure

Baby, It's Cold Outside

Love Don't Live Here Anymore, Book 1, 2

Every Time We Touch (A Wet Heat Novelette)

One Night Only- Love By Design Book 1

Cassian and Savannah Love By Design Book 2

Deidra's Love -Love By Design Book 3

Protecting Bria: Book 1

Protecting Chanel:Book 2

Protecting Yanira: Book 3

Haven: A Single Dad Romance

Sensual

Seek to Please: Book 1

Seek To Touch: Book 2

Seek To Bare:Book 3

Seek To Love: Book 4

Seek To Trust: Book 5

Seek To Earn: Book 6

Tease Me: Book 1

Promise Me: Book 1

## By Ava S.King

Thank you so much for reading and if you enjoyed the crazy ride and decide to leave a review we'd truly appreciate the support..

# 304 Publishing Company

We showcase authors writing Romance, Women's Fiction, Thriller, and Erotic.Along with Mystery, Suspense, Poetry, Beauty, and Style Books. Thank you for taking the time out to visit. Join our mailing list to stay updated with new releases and blog posts.

Printed in the USA
CPSIA information can be obtained
at www.ICGtesting.com
JSHW052122180424
61459JS00008B/90